Zion
Quest

Book 1
Second Edition

Le Anne Kemmish

Note: This novel is a work of fiction. Present day names,
characters, places, and incidents are either products of the
author's imagination or used fictitiously. Characters from the
Kemmish family who came over on the Good Ship Golconda
which sailed January 24, 1853 are in fact true persons. Journals are fiction, except for the events they describe are docu-
mented in the Author's family history, written by Nathan
Andrew Kemmish in the year 1902.

Cover and interior design: LeAnne Kemmish
Edited by Jennifer Lucas
Printed in the United States of America
First printing 2010
Second Edition

ISBN-9780-0-578-47803-6

To my mother, who told me if I didn't have all the facts, then make up a story. I took your advice.

To my children, I love you all and you inspire me.

To my husband, thank you for all your support. I love you from the beginning until forever.

CHAPTER 1

Rachael stood stiff and emotionless as she dragged her eyes away from the caskets of her parents deep in the earth. She had dressed in the appropriate black dress her aunt Jenny picked out, but her thoughts were far from appropriate.

As each person in the crowd of grieving family and friends wiped their eyes, cleared their throats, and sniffled, Rachael stared into the distance with controlled anger tucked deep in her heart. Of course, she must keep it together now, in front of these people, especially the Pastor that had sent her parents to their deaths.

Is it wrong to blame a church leader? Who do I really blame? All this is so wrong. My parents loved God. How could God, if He says He loves us, allow my parents to be murdered in their sleep when they were doing His work? Why didn't He protect them? Pastor Jim knew the risks they were taking going into the

Amazon. Why didn't he stop them? This wasn't supposed to happen. Now what am I going to do? I am alone...

Pastor Jim cleared his throat to get her attention. He nodded toward the yellow roses clenched in her hands.

Rachael stepped up to the gaping hole that held her parents side by side and dropped each flower onto a coffin then grabbed two handfuls of dirt, cold and damp in her hands, to sprinkle into the grave as Pastor Jim spoke of how we all came from dust and dust we shall return.

Rachael took a deep breath and held it to control the welling of emotions she could not process, she would process it later in her room, alone.

Alone. Don't think about that now. Rachael gulped down the lump in her throat and concentrated on letting out her breath as to not draw attention to herself. Aunt Jenny stood beside her, hunched over and weeping. Rachael had to block her and everyone else out or she would explode.

"Rest in peace, Nathan and Jessica. You will be missed," Pastor Jim ended the ceremony, and everyone turned toward the line of cars along the cemetery drive. There were hugs and consoling exchanges. Rachael just stood there at the head of her parents' graves not knowing what to do, frozen and numb. If she headed for the car right now everyone would bombard her with words she could not face. Questions like "What will you do now?" "Do you need anything?" A shudder traveled down her spine as she contemplated these questions. Rachael bowed her head, wrapped her arms around herself, and willed everyone to go away.

Aunt Jenny waited at a black rented Limo for her niece to compose herself. Rachael independent spirit developed early in her toddler years. She had been raised as an only child not for the lack of trying. Her parents loved children. After Rachael was born, they tried for another child, but the babies didn't survive, despite modern medicine.

Nathan and Jessica had been close to God their entire adult lives and never questioned why He had only blessed them with Rachael. They had seemed content to serve their local church, teach Sunday school, and raise their only daughter to know God.

After Rachael left home to go to college, Jessica's heart changed. Then this opportunity to travel to the Amazon as missionaries came up and they felt called. Jenny struggled to let her sister go, but Jessica and Nathan missed Rachael so much. Now, they were with the Lord and Rachael was doing the missing.

Sometimes anger welled up inside her for what losing Jessica and Nathan would do to Rachael's life. Her life would always have this void where her parents should have been. When she fell in love for the first time and got married, when she had her first baby, everything.

Did any of us think about that when Jessica told us she and Nathan were going to be missionaries in South America? Who would have thought they would never come back? This is a terrible tragedy, I'm not sure how any of us will get through this.

Jenny's thoughts strayed toward the "what if" that grief brings. She watched her sister's child at the gravesite and closed her eyes. Raising her face to the heavens, she vowed to God she would help Rachael. Despite Rachael's rejection of her church going childhood and choosing a secular university, she prayed Rachael would find God in all this. Jenny stood on the Bible's promise that children would come back to what they were raised in, but this? Losing her parents was hard to get over and not blame God.

Rachael left the gravesite with her head down, shuffling her feet through the fresh cut grass. It broke Jenny's heart to see her so low.

I could blame you a little too, God.

Jenny sobbed another quiet prayer for their pain and for Rachael's salvation as they climbed into the limousine, the driver turned toward her sister's old house.

Rachael sat staring out the window as the line of grave stones ended and houses replaced them in her view. She took a deep breath and let it out, she hadn't noticed the tension in her body until then. Aunt Jenny reached over and grabbed Rachael's hand. Rachael gave her aunt a little squeeze. Aunt Jenny's presence comforted her.

Uncle Ben must be riding in the other limo with Dad's family that flew in last night. Rachael thought, as they rode in silence just holding each other's hand lost in memories of the loved ones they had buried.

Rachael prepared herself as best she could for the next ordeal once they arrived at the house. Everyone would be talking about Nathan and Jessica, and what good people they were. What a shame they died so young.

"God, I wish this day was over," Rachael said through clenched teeth. She started to breath in great gulps of air, trying to hold onto what little control she had. Aunt Jenny reached for her, but Rachael pulled away and looked out the window when she saw a silent tear slip down her aunt's cheek, she must compose her thoughts.

As the limo pulled into the driveway, cars lined both sides of the street. Doors began to open and out poured friends and family, many of them Rachael didn't know. She assumed they belonged to her parent's church. She recognized a few of her father's family from pictures since they lived in Iowa and she hadn't seen them in years.

"Okay Rachael. Don't be childish and run away," she said under her breath as she got out of the car and the dreaded hugs began. She couldn't do it. With the looks of sadness and pity in their eyes everything began to unravel inside her. Maybe she should have let out some of this painful burden and allowed herself a good cry. The flood gates of her emotions felt about to burst and in front of everyone.

Aunt Jenny pulled her aside into the hallway near the door, away from earshot of the others.

"It's okay to cry, honey. I'm amazed at how you have kept it together this long. Go on up to your room if you need to. I will take care of things down here for now." That was all it took. Rachael ran to her room and closed the door. She threw herself across her bed, grabbed her pillow and cried into it. The anger in her exploded as her sobs turned to screams into her pillow.

The churning emotions subsided then more tears came, and plenty of them, then the hiccups. She cried until she felt in control again. She sat up and looked across the room at her reflection in the dressing table mirror. The wild haired, gaunt, red faced person staring back at her, she hardly recognized.

Rachael slid her feet over the side of the bed, swayed a bit before strength came back to her legs, then walked to the mirror. Bending to look closer at her face she wiped away the hair that was stuck to her tear dampened cheeks and went to the door. She had to face her guests, not her parent's guests, but hers. Rachael took a large breath, held it for a few seconds and let it out as she reached for the doorknob to face the future of so many unknowns.

CHAPTER 2

Rachael sat at the breakfast table, watching her mother at the stove serving up eggs and pancakes. She stared at her back memorizing every detail. Unbrushed waves of golden hair floated down her mother's back. Her mother wore her old slippers with broken-down heels, and a robe Rachael recalled smelling like her mom's home-made maple syrup.

Rachael jumped up from the table and raced to her mother with arms held wide to wrap around her waist, but when she reached out to touch her, the kitchen dissolved. Her mother disappeared as she woke up and realized it was a dream.

These dreams had become the norm since her parents' funeral. It had to be this house, everywhere she turned she saw, touched, and even smelled her mother. She'd learned in Psych class, before she left school, that smell was the strongest memory.

Psych class; Chemistry; English; all of which she dropped since her parents' death. What could she have done? There was too much to handle; the funeral, the will reading, deciding what to do with the house and the rest of her life without her mom and dad helping her make these tough decisions. The dean had offered to refund her tuition and keep her as an active student until she returned. At this point Rachael couldn't predict tomorrow, let alone when she would return to school.

First, I will deal with the house. Aunt Jenny will be here soon to help me decide what o keep and what to donate of Mom and Dad's things.

With the decision to get out of bed, Rachael threw back the colorful adolescent coverlet, swung her bare feet to the floor, and slid the rest of her tired body with them. She moved like she hadn't slept a wink for weeks, dragging her feet across the floor like a zombie and down the hall to the bathroom. She hesitated at her parents' closed bedroom door, listened out of years of habit, and moved on. Part of her still hoped she would hear the slight snoring of her father but most of her understood the reality and finality of their absence. Still, the part of her heart that did not understand stabbed at her every time she passed their room.

Ugg, I'm not looking forward to going through mom and dad's dressers and pack everything up for The Ark to pick up. Once that's done I want to go through the attic. I'm sure there's a lot I could donate from the piles up there. Rachael listed the chores storming around in her head like thunder clouds.

The attic held plenty of memories of her

mother. Rachael had spent hours with her making forts out of sheets and boxes, having tea parties with dolls and stuffed animals she drug up the stairs from her room. Sometimes she invited Sally down the street. They had played dress up with all the old clothes in the big trunk under the small sunny window. But now she was a grownup dealing with grown-up problems no nineteen-year-old should have to deal with.

*The only thing I should be worrying about is getting to class on time. If it were't for Aunt Jenny I couldn't ...*Pain in her chest stopped her thoughts as she pulled her arms around herself and dropped into the nearest chair at the bottom of the stairs; the physical pain from sadness and loss coursed through her like a wave. Rachael's heart shattered and there was nothing she could do about it but give in as wracking sobs took over.

She had put off the inevitable grieving but sitting in her mother's chair and looking around the room at all her mother's things made her wish she was a little girl again, who could crawl into her mother's arms to be rocked. Rachael pulled her bare feet up under her and drug the hand crocheted afghan off the back of the chair and rocked herself. She cried out loud because there was no one to hear her. She gave into the long painful sobs that shook her body. Her grief pressed down on her chest like a load of bricks that made it hard to breath.

"Why? Why did it have to be my parents?" She screamed with anger pouring out of her.

"They were such good people? God, why

did you take my Mom and Dad?" She wailed into the empty house.

In an instant the pain disappeared, and the tears dried up. She could breathe again. Peace replaced her anger. She found it strange that a moment ago her body was filled with pain and loneliness that she felt would never end; now it was gone. Confused, and only a bit freaked out by an overwhelming sense she wasn't alone in this house or in this world. Rachael sat up, took a deep breath, listening to the familiar creaks and settling sounds of the old house for noises out of the daily norm but nothing creepy or scary, and then let herself breathe out slowly.

Her mind started working again as if she needed that hard cry to get it out of her system. She looked at the clock on the mantle and realized Aunt Jenny would be there any minute. Rachael stood and wiped the remaining tears from her face. Her body still had the feel of a thousand pounds of sand pressing down upon her and she wanted to crawl back into bed, but she hoped breakfast and some coffee would revive her for another distressing day.

As she grabbed two cups from the cabinet above the gurgling coffee maker, she heard a knock on the back door to the kitchen. The door opened, and Aunt Jenny's face appeared around it. She looked at Rachael with eyes filled with sadness. Rachael rushed to her, and they held each other in the doorway not willing to let go just yet until their tears stopped falling.

"You want a cup of coffee before we tackle

the hard stuff?" Rachael asked wiping her tears on her sleeve, they walked across the sunny kitchen to the counter holding hands.

Handing her a steaming cup, Rachael noticed the dark puffiness under Aunt Jenny's hazel eyes. Despite that, she looked far too young to have two grown sons. Youthful skin ran in the family. The compliments her mother and Aunt Jenny would get when they were out in public used to embarrass her. People would think they were her sisters and not a generation older. Rachael compared her features to these two women, but the only similarities were her petite size and golden blond hair.

Rachael had inherited her deep blue eyes from her dad's side of the family. Most of them had dark hair and blue to blue-gray eyes but her father's family all lived in the Mid-West and she could remember only one visit when she was young. Grandpa Pete was the only one in the family who settled in Eastern Washington and he gave this house to her parents when he died. They had been married only a couple of years when Nathan and Jessica moved in to take care of Grandpa in his last days. Rachael hadn't been born yet.

Looking around the open floorplan of the country kitchen, Aunt Jenny envisioned two young sisters working side by side when she came for a long visit to help Jessica with the painting and fixing up of the old place. They became best friends through the process and closer than any sisters they knew. Because of that visit, when Ben retired from the Air Force, they moved to be near Jessica and Nathan. Now her best friend was gone forever but the daughter remained, and she still needed a mother. With her two sons grown and off on their own, one in the Air Force like his father, and the other married and teaching up in Alaska, Jenny vowed to be Rachael's mother from then on.

"Grab the garbage bags and let's get this over with," Aunt Jenny said, refilling her cup. She dribbled a bit of creamer in, and then headed to the bedrooms. "Did you call the Arc to see when they could pick up the stuff?"

"No, I wasn't sure when I would be ready for that," Rachael said, bowing her head away from Aunt Jenny's searching eyes.

"It's ok, honey, we'll get through this one step at a time." Jenny grabbed Rachael's hand and they walked together up the stairs to her parents' room.

"If there's anything you want, Aunt Jenny, just take it. I don't think I'm keeping anything in here," Rachael said over her shoulder, as she opened the closet and saw her mother's robe hanging on a hook inside the door.

"Except this," she said under her breath with a sigh, as the dream of her mother that morning flooded through her.

Rachael lifted the sky-blue terry robe off

the hook, brought it to her face and breathed in deep, then put it on. She swam in the scent of her mother and wrapped her arms around herself imagining being hugged. She would keep this one thing forever, and the thought made her heart soften.

Before lunch they were done with the bedroom and closet.

"After lunch we'll head for the attic. You want a toasted cheese sandwich and tomato soup, honey?" Aunt Jenny asked, with a funny smirk on her face. It was comforting to her that her aunt knew Rachael's favorite lunch when she was a little girl. A bit of hope slipped under the grief in her heart that gave her a moment where she thought she may get through another day with the help of her aunt Jenny.

CHAPTER 3

At the end of the walk-in closet, which now stood stark white in its emptiness, a narrow staircase led to the attic. The stiff, grinding old hinges creaked as Rachael pushed the door open and fumbled along the inside of the wall heading up the stairs for the pull string tied to a nail that turned on the light. The old bare bulb made a loud pop, as it went on then off again and they both jumped. She tried the string again, but the bulb must have burned out.

"Oh, I know where a flashlight is," Rachael said as she turned, bumping into Aunt Jenny standing close, on her way to her dad's nightstand. Back at the stairs she reached for Aunt Jenny's hand, only then realizing how creepy the attic at this moment as the beam of light swung to and fro, throwing shadows across the wall which illuminated the labyrinth of cobwebs.

"Do you feel like we have just entered into a scary movie?" Rachael asked over her shoulder and Aunt Jenny chuckled, squeezing her hand.

"There are better lights at the top of the stairs," Rachael whispered, still holding tight to Aunt Jenny and inching her way up one stair at a time. She wiped the cobwebs aside and trembled as the long strands of dusty web slipped over the raised hairs on her arms.

Where there are cobwebs there are spiders, not something I need to think about right now. I hate spiders more than anything.

Rachael could not control the shudders going through her body.

As they reached the top of the stairs Rachael flipped a switch nailed to the two by four framing of the unfinished attic, and light spread into every corner. A pale glow fell on the piles of memories her mother could not part with. In the corner near the stairs sat the fake Christmas tree covered with an old sheet. A stack of boxes marked Xmas Decorations written across the ends with a black marker, stood next to it.

Her eyes spotted the one thing she cherished most from her attic memories, the big steamer trunk her mother kept under the window, and there it was just as she remembered it. Voices and giggles seemed to fill the room. She relived special scenes as she rolled the dusty sheet away that covered it, being careful not to stir up the dust that might cause a fit of sneezing.

Rachael knelt in front of the trunk and ran her hands across the cracked leather stretched over the arched top. She traced the initials engraved above the latch. E. R. K.

It always made momma laugh when I would

say it was the erk trunk.

Rachael chuckled out loud.

Aunt Jenny knelt beside Rachael as she opened the big trunk with a creak of the old leather hinges. Rachael held her breath in anticipation.

She spied the layers of tissue-paper wrapped multi-colored fabrics stacked to one side of the trunk. Rachael lifted each package out one by one, careful not to disturb the delicate tissue.

"These are the old dresses I used to play in when I was a little girl." She told Aunt Jenny smiling. She continued emptying the trunk; a silver tea set tarnished and in desperate need of polish, an antique sword sheathed in its scabbard, a carved wooden jewelry box, a baby doll that had a crack along her beautiful porcelain face, a large sewing box, and several other boxes tied with faded ribbons. Rachael reached the bottom and patted around to make sure the old trunk was empty before she sat back and looked at Aunt Jenny.

"That's all of it. This was my favorite thing to do when I was a little girl, empty the trunk and play in it. I guess I never thought too much about what all this stuff was except the dresses." Lost in her childhood memories Rachael fingered a corner of satin fabric escaping from its protective tissue.

It surprised Aunt Jenny how much stuff Jessica had crammed into the attic. While Rachael was growing up, Jenny had traveled with Ben where ever the Airforce took him; to Germany then Italy then back East. She had missed all the early days of Rachael's childhood and her sister trying to have another baby, but they had kept in touch through phone calls and letters. The last miscarriage Jessica had, Jenny had flown back to help her, but could anyone really recover carrying a baby for six months then losing it? That was when she and Nathan decided to stop trying. It was just too much.

Without saying a thing, Jenny watched Rachael put the tea set back into the trunk along with the sword, porcelain doll, and sewing box. She opened the jewelry box and glanced inside for a moment before she shut it and put it in the trunk as well. Then she took the closest tied box, slid the ribbon off the end, and took the lid off. It contained letters stacked from one end to the other in two neat rows, small envelopes on one side and larger envelopes on the other. Rachael pushed the first one away from the edge of the box as Jenny read over her shoulder.

To: Elizabeth Kemmish, most of them said. Some were for a Charles, and others were for a Peter Charles and Eliza. Rachael was about to put the lid back on when Jenny glanced at the stamp.

"These are old letters; Dated back to the 1850's," Jenny said.

"Let's save these for tonight," Rachael suggested as she set the letter box aside and grabbed another, opening it. But this one had sheets of paper with fine lacy handwriting across the pages. Someone had bound the journals by sewing the pages together with thin twine.

Jenny had noticed the pages dated back to the mid 1800's and read like a journal, she assumed written by a woman. Jenny opened two other boxes of the same size filled with journals as well. Of course, they weren't signed because they were journals; a private collection of thoughts not intended for public viewing.

Rachael's heart pounded with the anticipation of what these boxes may contain, and it took her quite a bit of self-control to set them aside and start going through the other things stacked around the attic. While categorizing each pile she couldn't help her mind returning to the journals.

"Whoever wrote the journals must be an ancestor. I wonder who this woman was and how far back she is related to me." Rachael counted the dates back and the writer lived over one hundred fifty years ago. *That is a long time, maybe five or six generations.*

"I can't wait to read what it was like to live during that time?" Rachael rambled thinking out loud.

Rachael loved History and English, her favorite subjects in school. Because of her love of the past she had been working toward a teaching degree like her big cousin Sam whom she had always wished was her brother. She wanted to teach at the high school or college level. But that was on hold for now; she needed to work out where she fit into this new life without her parents, before she could start planning her future.

Under the eaves, to the left of the trunk, a cradle with dust covered toys Rachael had played with as a little girl sat almost unnoticed.

"Do you think Sam would want that cradle for the new baby?" Rachael asked Aunt Jenny pointing. Aunt Jenny was expecting her first grandbaby by Sam and his wife Shelley in the spring.

"Could be, I'll ask him when he calls next week."

The boxes piled in the other corner had old clothes in them. Rachael dragged them down to the front door for the Arc truck to take away. Several trips later Rachael looked around at the space as they emptied the attic. She'd love to set up her writing desk, easel, and canvas and make this room a studio just for her, then she realized the whole house was "just for her" now.

Rachael didn't need to sell the house, since it was paid for. She could transfer to the local university but that was too much to think about and too soon to plan. Her head began to pound from too much thinking or maybe the dust caused it.

Still, the trunk; the cradle and toys; the Christmas decorations and an old rocking chair with threadbare faded tapestry covering it; the box of letters; and the journals lay in organized disarray in the attic. These things Rachael decided to keep, but she wanted the trunk close to her in her room. Getting the heavy trunk down the narrow stairway was no easy task as first Aunt Jenny stumbled and then Rachael as they grunted, shoved and yelped in pain as they each took turns pinching their fingers between the trunk and the wall. Once in her parent's room Aunt Jenny and Rachael collapsed against the heavy trunk and caught their breath.

Rachael called Carl's Pizza a few blocks away to deliver so they didn't have to wait another minute before delving into the journals. Still wrapped in her mother's robe, Rachael piled the boxes on the bed. Aunt Jenny called Uncle Ben and put him on speaker, to let him know she was staying overnight.

"Do you two need anything?" He asked.

"We have pizza coming. Oh, we have entertainment too. We found these old journals in the attic that we'll be reading tonight so don't worry about us."

"Okay then, I'll bring breakfast over tomorrow morning." Rachael couldn't hold back a giggle as she watched Aunt Jenny roll her eyes.

"What kind of breakfast?" Aunt Jenny asked with her face twisted up in a wry smile.

"Just never you mind." Uncle Ben squeaked out through suppressed chuckles and hung up the phone.

"Cinnabon, again. I swear that man sweats cinnamon. I keep telling him those are bad for his health, but he takes every 'special occasion' to eat them," she said with her fingers up making air quotes. "Apparently, this is one of those moments," Aunt Jenny mumbled as she followed Rachael to the kitchen.

Rachael paid the delivery man and took the pizza to the bedroom.

"I'll get some sodas and paper towels," Aunt Jenny called from the kitchen then joined Rachael in the master bedroom. They snuggled under the big comforter on Nathan and Jessica's bed and settled down eating pizza, wiping their fingers, and reading. Aunt Jenny was more interested in the box of letters while Rachael grabbed the stack of journal boxes. She opened them and laid them out on the bed to determine which contained the first journal.

CHAPTER 4

*A*ugust 3rd, 1852

When Charles told me our dearest friends, the Kays, as well as fourteen other families from our district were going to America, my heart sank and leapt at the same time. I began this journal to keep my thoughts as well as document this great occasion for we decided to go to America with them. I will miss my family, but our faith calls us to Zion.

Francis and Lucretia Kay were the first friends we made once we became members of the Church of Jesus Christ of Latter Day Saints back in '48. Their children are the same age as our boys and are great friends for them. We have since dreamed of immigrating to Utah, the state chosen by Brother Smith to gather our faithful so that we could all prosper together in God and support one another. We call it Zion; Paradise; The Holy Land of our faith.

Charles took on the office of Secretary of our South-

ampton Conference and that is when he began assisting the Church with the immigration processes. He tells me there is much to be organized to accomplish such a great exodus of our people and to prepare a place for us in Utah. Ships are being rigged for the long trip over the Atlantic to leave by late fall. There is so much to do and so little time to do it in.

I am not sure how Liz and Janie will feel about this, but I am sure they will adjust in time. No matter, they go where we go.

August 15th, 1852

I have only a few minutes to write for there is much to do to prepare for the passage across the Atlantic. It will take two months, so we must make provisions for the long trip. There are dresses to sew for Elizabeth and Jane, short pants and shirts for the three boys who are growing so fast I do hope they won't be out of these before we sail. There are biscuits to bake and put up, beef to dry, fruit and vegetables to put up come harvest. Wheat; lard; yeast; corn meal; oatmeal; cheese to preserve, and fish to can; linens to sew; and so many other things I can not possibly think of right now. Thank the good Lord I have my two young ladies to help and though they cried and moped around the house for a week after we told them we were preparing for this adventure, they came around as I knew they would.

Janie is such an immense help with the boys, especially James, she will go about her chores with him se-

curely straddling her hip. I envision her being a mother of a dozen beautiful blue-eyed children in her lifetime. However, Elizabeth has not shown this same interest. Her nose is usually buried in her school lessons or reading a novel. She is very studious.

I went to the doctor yesterday and I am to have another child in the spring. I think I instinctively knew then when Charles came to tell me we were leaving on the next ship and that is why my heart jumped around in my chest so strongly. I guess I must find some way to prepare for this.

Rachael nudged Aunt Jenny "The woman who wrote this came over on a ship to America pregnant and listen to what she said.

'Charles wanted to postpone our departure until next year, since I am expecting, but I would have none of it. Women have been having babies since the beginning of time. I am sure this birth will be no different, only on American soil. Just imagine my good fortune to be having the first American in our family and that is exciting.'" Rachael read to her aunt.

"Wow, she had five children and another on the way, yet she still wanted to take a ship for two months," Aunt Jenny replied.

Aunt Jenny had read a few of Elizabeth's letters, and compared to the journal, they believed the journal writer was the same Elizabeth since the letters mentioned her children by name.

Rachael read on silently since Aunt Jenny moved her lips while reading the next letter from the box.

'I thank the good Lord I am not burdened with the morning vapors like many other women in my condition. Even though this is true, I do find myself tiring much sooner than I am accustomed and must lie down in the early afternoon for a respite. I take this resting time to catch up on my journaling. I must nap now though, I wrote more than I should. There is too much to do, I have no time to be an invalid.'

Putting aside the journal, Rachael's curiosity about the other unopened boxes got the better of her. She grabbed the next ribbon tied box which was long and narrow and opened it. The box had a card catalog like what you would find in an old library, only it had pictures with cardboard sections separating photos by dates. Rachael went to the date after the departure of the family to America and thumbed through until she found a photo with a husband, wife and nine children. Charles and Elizabeth, with all the children listed from left to right in neat but flowing handwriting. Young Elizabeth and her husband Hugh Moon; Jane and her husband Thomas Fowler; Peter Charles; Daniel; James Ephraim; Eliza Golconda; and Ruth.

In parentheses was a note (Rachel would have been here, but she died shortly before we took this picture – she was six. And the youngest is Elizabeth's child Sarah.)

"Hey, there was another Rachael in the family, but she died when she was six. This must have been taken several years after they immigrated to America." Rachael showed Aunt Jenny, pointing to each person and reading the names off the back.

As she read the names, Aunt Jenny's eyes widened. "They all look so young, and the oldest had a child already?" She took the picture from Rachael and looked closer.

"I guess that's how they did it in those days," Rachael said thumbing through the rest of the pictures. Several of pictures were of people who stood by wagons, fronts of old buildings, and many of the pictures had nothing written on the back. Then there was a whole section of postcards with people and places in Iowa dated many years after the family photo. Rachael will have to go over them later for she was falling asleep with all this piled on the bed.

Aunt Jenny took the box off Rachael's lap, put the lid and ribbon back on, and set it along with the others on the floor. With a sigh, Rachael slid under the covers. The last thing she heard was the click as her aunty turned off the light.

CHAPTER 5

Dark shadows moved through the trees around the makeshift straw huts scattered around a central fire pit in the middle of the jungle. The fire had dwindled down to smoking, bright red embers. A slight shuffling sound just outside the perimeter of the camp drew very little attention. Was it the wind in the giant philodendron leaves? The dark was filled with insects and night bird calls. The missionaries, sound asleep on their cots unaware of the danger lurking beyond their dreams as the dark shadows crept closer. Several of the huts had the rain shutters open to catch the slightest breeze.

Nathan and Jessica slept as only those comfortable with their lives secure in the Lord. Two cots slid together so they could sleep holding hands as they had done for twenty-two years of marriage. They slept inside a hanging bug net protecting them from many of the flying and crawling things in the jungle.

One of the dark shadows split off from the jungle and came into the room filled with sleeping sounds. As one, then the other sat up, Nathan then Jessica fell back down on their cots, their last breaths the only sound within the grass walls. The dark shadow took shape and there in the middle of the hut stood a warrior with grey paint across his face and bare chest. A long spear held in his hand, the tip red and dripping with the blood of the missionary couple he had been commissioned to sacrifice for the sake of his people.

He turned away from the beds where the couple lay lifeless. He peered out into the night and his face was devoid of any emotion, waiting for the signal that the others had accomplished their necessary deeds. He stared again into the still night air, then he saw her, their eyes met in the darkness. The assassin's eyes squinted then opened wide in disbelief. He raised his spear in readiness to attack.

Rachael looked into the eyes of her parent's murderer and screamed. She saw it all. She screamed and turned to run but she couldn't feel her legs. She screamed again when someone grabbed her arms and shook her. She heard her name and a light flicked on, dragging her from the nightmare. Rachael was lying in her parent's bed with Aunt Jenny standing over her, her face etched with concern. Rachael was covered in sweat and goose bumps.

"Honey, it was a dream. It's ok, wake up Rachael." Aunt Jenny crawled back under the covers and gathered Rachael into her arms. It took several minutes of rocking before she stopped crying and shaking.

"I saw him. I saw him." Rachael repeated until she calmed down enough to tell Aunt Jenny about her nightmare.

"He looked right at me as if I had been there. He had this look on his face, I don't know what it was, but it scared me so bad. I thought he was going to kill me too."

"Shhhh, Rachael, it was just a bad dream. It's natural for you to wonder what happened and your imagination filled in the blanks is all. I am going down to the kitchen and make us both some chamomile tea to settle us down." Aunt Jenny got out of bed, but before she left the room Rachael jumped up and dogged her steps to the kitchen.

"No way am I going to be alone, not after that awful dream." Rachael grabbed the sleeve of one of her mother's nightgowns Aunt Jenny was wearing and they both giggled but Rachael's laugh stopped short, being drawn back to the terror she endured only minutes ago.

Cups of fragrant herbal tea in their hands, they settled back in bed around three in the morning. Though she tried, Rachael could not get back to sleep. Once Aunt Jenny's breathing steadied, she slipped from bed and grabbed up the journal. Looking back, she noticed her rhythmic breathing never wavered.

Rachael tiptoed out the door and down the stairs, skipping the creaky stair second from the bottom. She sunk onto the big over stuffed loveseat in the corner of the living room and switched on the lamp on the side table.

Flipping the lid off the box she took the top journal out and studied the binding. The stitches spaced evenly across the binding impressed Rachael. Even back then someone had the skill and precision to do this well and by hand. She imagined Elizabeth back in England binding this book preparing to fill it with all the wonders of the new world she would travel to, a new life.

Rachael opened the journal to where she'd left off.

August 18th, 1852

Charles and the boys went out fishing this morning in the early hours before dawn. Peter Charles was so manly sporting his own fishing pole. I am proud of my boys taking on several more responsibilities in preparation for our journey. Whatever they bring home, Liz, Janie and I will smoke for the trip over sea and land.

Charles received a letter on the Packet this morning from Mr. Dennison who is the Immigration Agent handling matters in New Orleans. He sent a list of things we will need for the crossing and for the trek over land. Each family will need to have enough money to purchase all the items once we reach land. We will have to purchase our own wagons and oxen to pull them and horses to ride for the men and boys.

We are limited on what we can take on the ship. Though we are allowed one crate for our personal things and three crates for household items I am afraid we will not be taking any furnishings and I am sadder than I let on. These things of mine have been handed down through our family for generations. I have had to part with them to my sisters and brother. They will take loving care of them.

I have begun a mental list of my dearest things I must take along with the necessities. Though Charles will chide me for this frivolous fancy of mine I am a sentimental woman after all. I must make room for my grandmother's tea set she received as a wedding gift. How would we carry on our dear English customs without a tea pot? I refuse to serve high tea out of a tin can and Charles will just have to understand.

Janie is crushed that we will not be taking her piano. To console her, Liz put an arm around her young sister and said "It will be fine dearest. Now we will all be able to have some peace and quiet." We had difficulty not encouraging Liz in haranguing her sister. Janie has only played for a short while becoming quite a bit better lately. I reminded Liz of this, and she apologized to Janie, who took all in the beautiful spirit she takes most things.'

Rachael nodded off and slept for the rest of the night curled up in the corner of the short couch. She woke to Aunt Jenny grinding coffee in the kitchen. The journal lay open across her lap where she must have held it safe while sleeping, thankful that the rest of the night had no more nightmares.

"If sleeping sitting upright is the ticket for not having bad dreams then that's the deal," Rachael said, as she came around the corner into the kitchen still wearing her mother's blue robe hanging open with the tie trailing behind her.

"You look ready for coffee," Aunt Jenny chided as she straightened the robe and tied it for

Rachael. She grabbed the pot and poured a very dark cup of coffee for her young niece. Screwing up her nose, Rachael carried her cup to the fridge for the creamer.

"Have to have coffee with my creamer," Rachael joked holding up her mug. "Who could drink this stuff straight?" She poured a large amount of creamer into her cup and stirred it with a spoon Aunt Jenny had left on the counter.

"Uncle Ben will be here soon, and he is bringing breakfast. Well, what he thinks is breakfast," Aunt Jenny said with a smile and a raised eyebrow. Rachael's mouth watered in anticipation for the cinnamon rolls her uncle loved and took every opportunity to pick up despite Aunt Jenny's nagging.

Sipping coffee with her fingers curved around the large warm mug, Rachael shuddered. That dream still haunted her even in the day light, but a noise on the back porch drew her attention away with a shake of her head, then the back door opened. Sure enough, Uncle Ben came in with the familiar Cinnabon box in his hands and broke the spell.

CHAPTER 6

Azuno sat up from his mat across the fire pit from his father in the early morning hours drenched in sweat from the dream he had of the ugly business at the missionary camp. He glanced across at his sleeping father's form and determined that he was unaware of Azuno's distress at the dream.

Her eyes were still strong in his memory, blue as the sky and big with shock and fear at seeing him there.

Did she see what I had done? Who was she? It couldn't be real but Azuno could not shake the thought that she had seen everything.

Azuno reenacted what happened that night in his mind as he stared at the wall of his hut. He saw nothing out of place from what he and his father had planned that night. Yet, when he had made the signal to leave the missionary camp, the only movement he noticed were the other warriors he had brought with him. His mind must be playing tricks on him and he would speak to his father about asking the Ancestors for clarification. His father was a great Shaman as he too will be some day.

Azuno laid back on his mat after he adjusted the water bladder over the coals and stoked the fire to start the morning tea his father would want when he awoke.

Father understands everything. He knew the mission people were coming and he knew they were bad for his people. When the people began to disappear, Father asked the Ancestors what to do and they told him his people were being taken as slaves and they will lose their souls to the missionary God. That is when Father gathered the other warriors to assist me in stopping the taking of our people. It was necessary. Azuno busied himself with breakfast to try and forget about the missionaries and the dream.

Throughout the day he searched the village for any sign of the mission people, but all was as before. He forced the blue eyes from his mind. Later that day, by the time of the evening gathering for the communal supper, he still hadn't had a chance to speak to his father. His Shaman duties kept him busy healing and caring for his people's physical and spiritual well-being. His father took his responsibility of the Yanomami people's safety to the point of ordering the elimination of any threat.

Azuno remembered when the people called his father Dabun, the name his mother had given him. But now, they called him Shazundo. It had been fitting for Azuno to call him Father until his manhood ceremony, but in his mind, he could not change what he had done all his life. Even though his father had not corrected him in private, Azuno took care not to address him in such familiar terms in public.

For generations, even from the beginning of history, each Shaman learned to reach back in time to glean the wisdom and knowledge of the Shamans before him. Azuno's father had told him that soon it would be his turn to train in this special ceremony, then he would go through the preparation and the transference of his father's powers to him. At that time Azuno would receive a new name as well. Not yet, though, as Azuno well knew, for his father's power and influence throughout the region continued.

Other tribes from several days travel would send for him to heal or invoke the spirits on behalf of one person or a whole village. Sometimes the look on his father's face when he returned frightened Azuno as the Shaman would barricade himself in his ritual hut for hours then return looking like his father again. Having the strength to fight for his people took courage that his father thought he was not ready for, but the very act against the mission people had brought him one step closer in Shazundo's eyes.

Finally, after the evening meal and the sunset glowed in the western sky, father and son headed for their hut. Azuno told his father what he had dreamt. Long after settling down near the fire pit, Shazundo stayed quiet after Azuno finished. Azuno had been taught at an early age to sit quietly and not make a sound while his father conversed with the Ancestors. He learned that to make a sound would turn the Ancestors on him and cause great torment to his body and soul. He had fallen into a fever that shook him for days before he begged his father and the Ancestors to forgive his disobedience. He never made a move or sound again when his father visited in the spirit world.

It seemed like an eternity, Azuno heard a long sigh come from his father's lips as he turned his face toward his son. The Shaman reached out and put his hand on Azuno's strong, youthful shoulder as he steadied himself.

"Come; let us rest for a bit while the night tea steeps, then we will talk." Shazundo groaned as he repositioned himself closer to the fire preparing the evening herbals that would help him sleep and aid in the easing of the pain in his old bones.

Azuno's anxiety for what the Ancestors may wish him to do next played up and down his spine, but he showed no sign of weakness in front of his father. The last man who had trained to take the old man's place questioned him on the wisdom of some minor thing and the next day the villagers found him dead, his face and hands as black as night.

His father told him later that no one questioned the Ancestors and to anyone who was foolish enough to do so would bear the consequences. That same day, Shazundo informed Azuno he would take the place of the man who died. Still a boy then, but soon to be a man at the next summer ceremonies. That was two summers ago and Azuno still waited for the time he began his apprenticeship.

As the Shaman sipped his tea he spoke of what would be done.

"The blue eyes you spoke of from your dream, you say, were a woman's?"

Azuno nodded.

"She is the child of the mission people. She has great power to see you from such a distance as this. You are in danger of losing your soul to her even at this distance. Be strong my son, you must journey and seek out this demon who wishes to take your spirit away from you. You must fly to the land of the mission people and bring her back here so that the Ancestors can break the bond they have on our people. This says the Ancestors." The Shaman fell silent and stared into his cup of herbs.

Azuno's heart pounded and his head reeled from what he had just heard. This cannot be possible. How could he accomplish such a task since he had not the confidence nor the knowledge of these mission people, their strange language, let alone where they once lived before traveling here. How would he learn all he needed and so quickly?

Before he could speak these doubts, his father answered his questions. "You are to go to Boa Vista and ask for Kumata. She will teach you the language of the mission people. Then you will be ready. You will go tomorrow. And when you return, the Ancestors say you will be ready to join me at the transfer ceremony. Now we sleep."

Without one more word Azuno's father got up from the fire and went to his sleeping mat, carrying his clay tea cup, sipping the strong herbal drink as he prepared for bed. Not one word that next morning as he assisted his son to pack his meager belongings in a pouch he slung over one shoulder.

The Shaman led the way through the village wearing his official ritual cloak, everyone watched, knowing their leader's son was heading out alone. Though they didn't understand why, they had wisdom enough not to question. As they reached the edge of the village the Shaman stopped, turned to his son and took him in his arms as a father would.

"Azuno, it will take you many days to reach the city. Go to Saaju, he will take you the rest of the way."

Shazundo then pushed his son to his knees and laid both hands on his shoulders. He repeated an incantation three times for safety and for the strength of all the warriors who stood and fought for the people before him to enter his son. These warrior guides would strengthen him on his long journey.

"Azuno, you must not fail for if you do, you will take
the place of the Blue Eyes and die for your people to appease the Ancestors." Azuno's body began to quake with the burden of his mission as his father looked deep into his eyes. Azuno sensed a great sadness as though Shazundo saw something of Azuno's future that disturbed him.

And then he disappeared. Azuno turned to say good-bye but he had gone.

Alone, and much more frightened than when he crept through the jungle to save his people from the missionaries. Frightened by the lack of skills to protect himself from this evil, confronting the evil in the missionaries own villages surrounded by the enemy. How would he be able to slip through this unfamiliar land unseen like he had through his own beloved world?

He would not have the strength of the jungle spirits. He would be alone. He feared the blue-eyed demon who wanted his soul. He feared he would die in this demon world full of blue eyes. How would he find that very one he feared the most? His dark thoughts whirred around in his mind like a torrential wind. Distracted by so many unknowns, he covered the two miles to Saaju's village without notice.

All their lives, Saaju and Azuno traveled between their villages and beyond hunting and trading. They traveled on streams that emptied out into the Mucajai River, in a canoe gouged out of a great kapok tree that grew strong and plentiful in the jungles of the Amazon they lived in.

They once traveled for ten days this way, either gliding with the current that took the water to meet the great river or carrying the canoe over land to the next stream in the direction of Boa Vista, many miles from Azuno's village. The two strong young men could paddle several miles, but when they traveled overland, the journey became arduous, navigating the carried canoe through the thick trees and underbrush of the jungles of Northern Brazil to the next water way.

Many days later Azuno finally reached the city. He took the note his father had put in his pouch before leaving their hut and read the directions to Kumata's home. The note contained a message for her and instructions for Azuno's education to fit into the mission people's world.

After deciphering her Shaman's note, the look on Kumata' face had not comforted Azuno. He knew her history with her father. Kumata had been educated by the mission people but fell very ill and Shazundo had healed her. Thankful for the Shaman for rescuing her soul before she was lost forever she owed much to Azuno's father.

While Azuno learned English, Kumata researched the names of the mission people so as not to attract attention to Azuno. She sensed he had something to do with the recent deaths because the note commanded her to find out everything she could about these people and their families in the US.

For years Kumata had mingled with the teachers if English, they trusted her believing she had been converted, not knowing what conspired after her sickness. This gave her ample opportunity to gather the information for Azuno's journey to the US and an in to get the needed documents for him.

Even though a motivated pupil, Azuno still

took a few months to learn enough before Kumata decided the time had come for the next step. She used the money the Shaman sent her for his journey to the US and bought new American clothes and shoes, a passport, and an airplane ticket to the city she was sure he needed to be in to find the one he was looking for.

Azuno had been in the hut of the only married couple that had come to Azuno's village. Kumata managed to narrow the search and found an address the missionaries sent letters to. A letter for this couple still waited at the post office and she snatched it while no one was looking. What luck, Kumata told Azuno that night when she handed him the letter from the blue-eyed demon he must destroy.

CHAPTER 7

Rachael had gained a sense of strength to become independent again, but it seemed to her a long, arduous journey, as she navigated through her grief in the days after her parent's funeral. She took only a few weeks to get the house in order and settle many of the financial issues. Thanks to Roger, her parent's accountant she had known since she bounced on his knee during tax season as a little girl, he had everything organized and only needed her signature.

She rubbed her temples, thoroughly confused as to everything he said but he assured her she could go back to school the winter quarter and not worry about finances. Her parents had made ample provision for her in their plans.

While grieving she had dreaded the inevitable face to face with Pastor Jim. He and his wife came over unexpectedly one afternoon to drop off some casseroles church members had made for her. Rachael had difficulty keeping to herself what she thought about Pastor Jim and his encouragement of her parents being missionaries. She blurted out her anger and frustration with God taking her parents.

They spoke for an hour and listened to Rachael's angry feelings, spoke of the mysteries of God and yes, her loss was tragic and senseless. And, that sometimes, it was impossible for us to understand the reasons terrible things happen to good people.

"I find, when I am faced with such devastating situations, I try and remember we cannot know all that will come out of this tragedy," Sarah, Pastor Jim's wife, said, reaching to give Rachael's tight clenched hands in her lap a gentle squeeze. "I lost my parents in a car crash when I was 26."

A scripture Pastor Jim quoted made Rachael scrunch up her face in disbelief, something like 'God works all things to the good for those who love him'. Rachael struggled to think what good could come from losing her parents and never having them with her again, but she acted cordial to the Pastor and his wife, yet relief flooded through her when they both stood and left with the proper 'Please let us know if we can help you in any way'.

When they finally left, Rachael leaned her forehead against the dark stained wood of the old front door and sighed. The now familiar anger welled up inside her again and she made a face toward the closed door. She wanted to blame them for everything.

Rachael needed to blame someone, and it

seemed the Pastor and his wife may be the best candidates, but deep in the recesses of her heart she knew she couldn't make it stick. Their concern for her seemed genuine.

"I suppose it's not their fault I'm alone," she muttered to herself. She decided to forgive them and let go of the anger she still carried. Knowing her parents, the way she did, if they didn't want to go they would have stayed home.

Though her reluctance to close the house and head back to her life was strong, she decided she couldn't hide out forever. As she drove back across the state to Western Washington University she had a lot of time to think about her future. The break in her studies left her a quarter behind, but she planned to catch up over summer session. Her greatest worry, what she would say to her friends or if she had any friends left at school. She hoped they would not act weird around her now.

Maybe she would be too weird for them since Rachael underwent quite a bit of emotional growth after what she had gone through these past few months recovering from her parents' deaths. No other friend she knew had needed to do this. How could they ever understand her now?

All the arrangements, when she started school, had been taken care of by her dad, now it was up to her. It would be easier to stay on campus than at home all summer in the house, alone without her parents, even though she would miss Aunt Jenny and Uncle Ben.

Her Aunt and Uncle expected their first grand baby by Sam and Shelley in Alaska in the spring. Aunt Jenny planned to stay with the new parents before and after the birth to help so she wouldn't be at home anyway. Rachael would miss her parents less if she buried herself deep in her school studies and social life at Western.

Once Rachael arrived back at school, re-entering went smooth, so much so she began to be suspicious that they were expecting her. She easily enrolled into all three of the classes she needed. A dorm room, a single at that, had been assigned to her already. Almost as if she had a university fairy god person. Life got back into a semblance of normal where Rachael found herself beginning to laugh again with her friends.

When Rachael had some down time, she would take the journal box from the bottom drawer of her desk under the window in her dorm room and read over the familiar handwriting of her Elizabeth. She started calling Elizabeth this when she realized how much she resembled her pioneering and independent ancestor. Through reading the journal she found out that Elizabeth's middle name was Rachael and the trunk belonged to her, thus the initials E.R.K.

Rachael started looking for other clues that proved blood was thicker than water. Reading through the perils Elizabeth managed to endure taught Rachael that she could do anything life threw at her, even aloneness.

As she sat in Geometry class Rachael day dreamed out the window remembering what she had read the night before of Elizabeth on the ship Golconda.

January 30th, 1853

Oh, my dear Lord, I never realized the extent of suffering a woman can go through on a rocking ship while with child. It is as if I am on one and one is in me. With every sway to and fro the water protecting the babe rocks to and fro as well. We have only been on the Golconda for 6 days, but it feels an eternity. However uncomfortable I am, I trust our good Lord will see me through.

Liz and Janie do what they can to comfort me and keep the boys occupied but I have little strength since eating is out of the question until the sea lessons in the swells that never cease in coming.

The ship's doctor informs me I will soon adjust to the movement and will feel right as rain again in no time. He encourages me to try and come up on deck every day for seeing the sky and the horizon will aid in my recovery. I must believe him so up I go now. My dear husband went earlier and said he will have a comfortable place made for me should I make it that far.

Rachael wanted a love like that. Charles seemed very devoted to her. She had read an earlier journal entry, weeks ago, that before they sailed they had visited the grave sites of their first two children Sarah and John who were buried in the soil of their native country Whales and was part of the reason they wanted a new life in a new country.

Sarah had contracted scarlet fever when she was three years old. She recovered, or so they thought, but her heart never healed, and she died two months later. John had a different story, his wild and reckless behavior, while at the wharf with his father, claimed his life. He climbed some rigging of a ship in dry dock, slipped and fell, hitting his head and died instantly.

The province where they lived, the school where John attended, the friends that watched them pass by with such sad faces had reminded her daily of her loss. Rachael understood Elizabeth and Charles's decision to leave them behind. They found it best to look to the future which taught Rachael she could tackle her life with great tenacity Elizabeth showed facing such obstacles.

Elizabeth suffered greater losses and recovered from far worse things than what Rachael had endured losing her parents. Rachael imagined losing a child but couldn't fathom the grief it would bring. She hoped she never would, even though it seemed her mother had gone through this as well. Her mother never mentioned it, but Aunt Jenny had let it slip one day as they were going over last-minute plans before Rachael went back to school.

It amazed her, the courage of the woman's spirit to not be crushed by the world's ugliness, the many tragedies women faced, generation after generation to this day. Because of Elizabeth's story Rachael had been rethinking her major toward women's studies, maybe becoming a counselor to help other women realize their strength in getting through the many complicated challenges of this age.

Drawing herself back to the present, Rachael realized the teacher had been giving instructions about an upcoming test. With a frustrated sigh escaping her lips, she vowed to herself to pay better attention. The bell rang, and she hurried to the Math lab knowing they had the information she missed from class and what she needed to study for the coming test.

As she walked the paved paths between buildings, Rachael gnawed at the idea of dropping Geometry. A week into the winter quarter and already she found Geometry to be complicated and boring. The teacher spoke in monotones and kept his back to the class. To pass this class she would need to stop staring out the window, wanting to be anywhere else. However, because of that she realized she would fall behind and need to spend time in the Math Lab getting help. When she reached the counter and asked the tutor if he knew what she needed to study for the next test she heard a man's voice behind her.

"I too question this," he said in a heavy accent she had never heard before. Rachael turned with a smile on her face and their eyes met. His eyes were almond shaped and dark. The smile on her face vanished but his never wavered. At least she thought he smiled though she noticed it didn't reach his eyes. Rachael pondered to herself which, genuine or pasted on for show.

"I am Azuno. You?" He asked Rachael reaching out to shake her hand.

Rachael turned to the student behind the counter, hoping he would break the uncomfortable silence and give her a chance to think. Had she seen this guy on campus before? She couldn't be sure, but he seemed familiar though she hadn't met him. She would have remembered.

She looked back at him and he smiled again. Rachael studied him from behind her lashes with quick glances in his direction. He had short cropped black hair, a cotton polo shirt and jeans with high-top converse shoes. Very normal for an American boy, not with that accent. She decided to give him the benefit of the doubt but not give him her name and smiled back at him. They both asked questions and got their answers from the math tutor and left.

Rachael surprised herself when she blurted she had to get to class when it was evident this guy wanted to chat, but his accent made her nervous and she didn't know why.

What name did he say? Aso, or something like that, she had difficulty understanding his English with the accent.

She hadn't thought she could be prejudice, but foreigners frightened her since her parents' deaths and with good reason. She glanced over her shoulder. He stood in the middle of the sidewalk watching her walk away. A shudder went through her and she rushed around the corner of the building. Out of his sight, she ran. She dodged into one building only to go out the doors on the other side. Her heart hammered against her ribs, so hard she thought it was going to burst out of her chest.

She leaned against a red brick wall, outside the Liberal Arts building she had raced through, to catch her breath and heard a quiet voice whisper in her head.

"Child do not be troubled?"

Rachael's breathing and heart slowed to normal. She questioned what she had heard and the peace this voice brought to her while she walked into her dorm building through the back door. That same peace she had experienced while at her home washed over her, calming her body and mind.

After Rachael finished her Geometry homework she studied for a History test. She was good at History, so it didn't take very long. Still wound up from that odd experience with the guy at the Math Lab, she decided to take the journal to bed and read until she fell asleep.

February 17, 1953
I am pleased to announce, with no little effort, Eliza Golconda Kemmish was born this morning, but not on American soil and this saddens me to no end. She is the tiniest of all little cherubs, but her eyes are as bright and quick

as any of my children ever were at her age.

I do believe she came sooner than she should but because of my inability to keep much sustenance down on this voyage she must have gotten severely frustrated at me and decided to find her nourishment elsewhere. The poor sweet babe, I am quite worried about her being so soon when we were not expecting her for another six weeks or so. I am hoping my doctor back in Southsea had been off a bit in his calculation of her due date. I just pray for her little soul to keep through this voyage. If she should thrive, she will be the most robust of us all.

March 21, 53 Arrived at New Orleans

We are saved! Oh Lord, you are good to your servants. Because of a storm our ship's captain ordered all of us into the hold where we sleep. We were locked in as if we were cattle without a lantern. We cried out for mercy but the sailors that took the lamps explained it was for our safety. Should they fall off their hook and break the ship would catch fire and we would all be lost. But, without them the hold was pitch black.

I believe I understand now but during the storm when I did not know if the screaming and clinging bodies were in deed my own children or if they were somewhere out in the storm being tossed about like bales of cotton on the sea. It was so dark who could tell.

The terror we all felt when a crack of thunder rattled our nerves along with the shuddering and cracking of the ship itself. The ship tipped so hard to its side we all began to slide into each other. Jostled end over end we rolled along with our bedding into a heap of arms and legs against one wall. The screaming in the dark pit of the hold was such a din, my babies clinging to every part of my aching body, the newborn babe wrapped in my shawl and tied to my breast in hopes that I or someone else may not crush her tiny little form, and myself, clinging for all our lives to the rough, splintering post I found in the dark that kept the ships deck from crushing us. I was nearly faint with it all when from the din I heard a shrill voice cry out "Sister Kemmish, shan't we pray?"

Oh, my Lord, I was tested and forgive this frail human her failings, but I was not gracious in my response to her. I yelled back with no sparing of sarcasm, "It is not a time to pray but to hold on."

The embarrassment of this statement will follow me to my grave, for the darkness became silent except for the storm while everyone contemplated my words. Liz, in her gracious way of coming forth with the truth, told me what I had said for I do believe I had fainted shortly after that and was revived by my dear Charles when the storm was over.

Soon after, we were informed we had reached the Gulf of Mexico where we encountered the hurricane that nearly sent us to the bottom of the sea. The main mast was despoiled at the very last portion of the storm and that is what nearly capsized us, yet the sailors were able to chop it free of the ship before it dragged us under.

I do believe I would have been better off not knowing this and I think my fainting was a blessing from God, not to mention I was malnourished and still weak from Eliza's birth. However, we had several weeks of ship reconstruction and calm weather before we were able to cross the sand bar at the mouth of the Mississippi and sail up the wide river to New Orleans.

I am happy to be back on solid ground; Eliza and I are gaining strength every day. Charles wants to be sure I *am strong enough to travel for it is a hard journey over rough territory and he prays hourly by my bedside so that I make it there alive. I must be well before our party sets out, otherwise we would have to wait for the next ship and I am not prepared to do that.*

Charles was so concerned for me after the storm he never left my side for days until I finally informed him that I must have respite from his face. I am glad he laughed at that, but it was no jest.

Rachael roared with laughter after reading that last comment. So true. Being an independent spirit and associating mostly in adult circles as an only child, she had difficulty sometimes relating to teenagers her own age. And, when she began dating at sixteen, she would shake her head at the young men who would pick her up at her home. Once in the car, they would turn up the stereo so loud they couldn't talk, while she thought it would be a wonderful opportunity to get to know them.

What was that all about anyway?

She supposed that being brought up as an only child where her parents treated her as an equal must be the main reason why she had not related to her fellow students in high school. The college boys she had met managed to be a little better, but she had not found nor even wanted to find a guy that interested her. Her dedication to her studies allowed her an excuse not to bother with them. Besides, difficult as it may be, she wanted to find someone as good and wonderful as her daddy.

These thoughts surprised Rachael. She had always thought her parents so out of touch with the real world, with their God this and God that, but reading how Elizabeth thanked God for everything made her think that maybe they weren't as far off as she had thought. She continued thinking about her parents and Elizabeth's relationship with God as she set the journal back into its box and placed it on her night stand. It seemed they had a relationship or something with this all powerful.... someone... they called Lord and Father. She turned off the light and snuggled under her down comforter making a mental list of the things she knew about God which seemed to her to be a bit too short.

CHAPTER 8

Azuno watched the blue-eyed girl walk away. He sought a silent answer from the Ancestors as he stood there on the sidewalk outside the Math Lab. Since his father invoked the spirits to aid in this quest he had heard many voices in his head as to what he must do. Sometimes, the voices clambered so loud and invaded every recess of his mind. He slept very little. As he stood watching her walk away and waited for an answer, none came.

He could not be sure he had found the one he had been looking for, there were thousands of young women on campus, and in this city, with blue eyes very similar to the ones he saw in his dream. The silence troubled him even more than the argumentative voices, he wondered what this meant. The overwhelming task caused his shoulders to slump.

Frustrated, and out of his element, he walked to his tiny apartment off campus and toward the part of town he could afford on the meager monies sent to him monthly by his father. He lived among many other students in his same financial position. It had been difficult surviving on the income, so he had found a job working a few mornings a week as a dishwasher at a breakfast place around the corner from his apartment.

A scholarship he earned paid his tuition and purchased his books. It specifically attracted bright young foreign students who otherwise would not be able to afford a college education. The students could study economics, engineering, and medicine so they could return to their homes and improve the overall wellbeing of the people in their communities.

He enjoyed his classes, leaning toward medicine in that he will be taking on his father's role as Shaman. However, much of his studies ran contrary to what he had been taught by his father so far. Bringing these current ideas home to his father, and to the Ancestors in particular, worried him, remembering what happened to the last apprentice.

When he thought on these things his head began to pound as if someone used his brain as a drum, possible, what with the warriors clambering around in there. It amazed Azuno that he could get any studying done at all with these complications beyond his control.

Back in his room, he had difficulty choosing between calling on the Ancestors and doing his homework. He must find this girl so that he could finally be at peace, but he knew once he did find her he would be returning home. He chose to study now and worry about the girl later.

Unzipping his backpack, he placed his books onto the furnished table in the kitchenette. He put water on to boil for his evening meal and smiled. He thought back to the first day in his studio apartment. He had to ask the landlord to explain all the odd items in each room.

His landlord rented to several students through the same program Azuno enrolled in and assisted these students in overcoming the culture shock when they were shown their rooms. Things like Refrigerator, Stove, Shower, Sink, running water, and Toilet were unfamiliar to him.

Even though he had gone to school for two months in Boa Vista, which had more modern amenities, it did not compare to the extravagance of the U.S. His apartment had all the furnishings he needed to be comfortable, however, most seemed too much and overwhelmed him.

After Azuno cooked his polenta and eggplant, he settled down at the table for a long night of Algebra, Biology, and English as a Second Language. He grasped the concepts of Algebra and Biology, he related each idea to what he knew from the jungles of Brazil. However, he found English complicated. He had only been speaking it for the past six months.

Saving English for last, he prepared for sleep then took his homework to a sleeping mat he fashioned on the floor next to the bed. After his first night in that bed he found it much too soft and high off the floor for his comfort. That night he fell out of it after a bad dream about being suffocated by clouds and woke up floating through the air then had the wind knocked out of him when he hit the floor on his back.

Through the difficult reading he needed to pass his English class he slid into a deep sleep with the book across his chest. His sleep became fitful as he found himself running through a familiar jungle.

Instead of freedom and confidence, his heart thundered inside his chest, in fright. He looked back behind him often, feeling a predator at his heels, but he saw nothing. Just as his lungs ached for him to rest, he came to a clearing where a large bonfire illuminated the scene. Men circled the flames, dancing in some ritual. Drums beating a hypnotic rhythm.

Azuno watched as two warriors dragged someone from his father's ritual hut toward the circle, with a blanket flung over the head obscuring any identifying features. The small form pulled against the strong arms that held tight. Then he saw her as the cloth slipped off and her golden hair swayed back and forth as if in a trance in the soft light of the fire. She struggled to get free.

He saw her deep blue eyes dart around the clearing, searching for salvation, but there was none who could save her. She looked past Azuno and he realized he was dressed as the others. She did not recognize him, but he recognized her from the Math Lab. His breath caught in his throat loud enough that his father turned to look at him. Everything stopped as their gaze locked onto each other.

His father's eyes pierced him like daggers and Azuno turned his face away in shame. He must have failed him somehow. If he had failed, then how did she get there? He did not know this. When the girl screamed, Azuno's head jerked up to see his father bring from his ceremonial robe a sharp curved blade over her head.

"NO!" Azuno shouted in English as he rushed to protect the blue-eyed American girl and the blade cut into him instead.

The piercing pain woke him, and he found himself sitting against the wall of his tiny apartment with a bright red welt across his chest. His breathing slowed as he listened for the intruder that could have done this to him. A sinking and perilous feeling came over him as he sat there in the dark of his bedroom.

You must do as you are told, or you will die in her place.

A quiet voice in his head spoke to him. The truth dawned in his heart, for he had seen the mysterious deaths in his village growing up. He must find this girl and take her to his father, so she would follow her parents to the spirit world where she could do no more harm to him or his people.

He spoke out loud in his native tongue so the spirits who brought this message would hear.

"Ancestors guide me then to the girl so that I will be sure to choose the right one. Make it so and let us be done with this business."

A wind and a high-pitched, whistling screech throughout the room spun his homework into a tiny tornado, scattering the pages across the room, then silence. The hair on the back of Azuno's neck bristled on his skin. There would be no sleep for him tonight.

He paced his apartment until dawn devising a plan for finding her with the help of the Ancestors. They would lead him to her. He planned to befriend her, so she would willingly get to know him. Then, somehow abduct her and take her to his jungle. After he completed this messy business he looked forward to being free to return to his studies. Free of his obligation to his father.

The winter quarter had only a few weeks left to completion. He would finish this ugly business over the break and be back before anyone missed him. Every other student went home or other places at spring break. No one will question where he went.

As the sun peeked through the blinds on his window, he gathered the strewn English papers and loaded his backpack to prepare for another day of classes. Azuno headed out with a fresh determination to concentrate on the ancestor's guidance to find the girl with the blue eyes who stole into his dream, trying to keep him from accomplishing his quest.

As he walked he surmised that through only a few months in this strange world, he had fallen into her trap by the enticing lure of his academics and letting go of the only reason he had come. His father was right, she must die or everything he knew of his people would die instead. He would not lose sight of that again and he silently pleaded for forgiveness from the Ancestors as he rubbed his chest where his reminder still pained him.

Instead of going to his classes he went straight to the Math Lab and chose a study cubicle in the corner where he could scan the room. He chanted under his breath the songs and phrases his father used to call the Ancestors to help him and waited.

He closed his blood-shot eyes to recollect what the girl in both dreams looked like. He had a better chance remembering last night's dream, being fresh in his memory. She looked smaller than the men who held her and since the men in his village tend to be shorter than most male students he had met, she must be quite short as well. Of course, blue eyes, and he saw in his dream golden hair shining in the fire light so in daylight it could be much lighter. He visualized blue eyes and yellow hair on a little body and sought that type of woman. Azuno knew her name from the letter for the dead couple, now he only needed to match that name with a face and then on to the next phase of his mission.

He had not waited long when the girl he spoke to yesterday came through the door and signed in for a tutor. She then sat at one of the round tables in the middle of the room to wait for help. She opened her Geometry book, pulled out a sheet of paper from a binder and started working with her head bowed over her book.

Azuno stood and walked around the lab desk behind her back and acted like he too needed to sign in, focusing on the name she had written. Inside his head a whirring sound began as he read Rachael Kemmish written neatly across the line with the date and time. He had found the woman. His heart jumped in his chest as he turned and stared at her. He found the blue eyed blonde-haired demon he had been sent after. Now he must pursue this woman as he had seen the men in the village during courting season.

In his culture the woman chose whom she married even though the men had more than one wife. Because of this, the men developed great means of persuasion and learned from an early age what women wanted in a husband. It had been this way from time eternal; from the beginning nothing had ever changed this. Even when the mission people came and told them to stop this damaging practice, the people in the village scoffed at these odd notions.

It is right for our people and because of this, most of his tribe found it difficult to believe anything else the mission people said about there being only one god and only one savior. What is a savior any-way? Perhaps a warrior spirit. What could it possibly be, this savior? Azuno had many questions about these white demon's beliefs.

Despite the questions and all the strange notions many left the village. That had to stop. There had to be an end to the stealing of souls or there would be no one left to carry on the traditions of the people. And if that happened the Ancestors would kill every one of the village people, his father told him so. Several families had already left our village to live in Boa Vista and be taught the missionary ways. Azuno saw them living, breathing, smiling when he learned English. It looked to him like they were alive and well which troubled him. Even without souls they looked just as if they still had not lost them.

Azuno picked up the pen Rachael had used and with a shaking hand he wrote his name on the next line then sat at Rachael's table, opened his algebra book to the page he had been working on the night before and waited.

Rachael looked up with a polite smile of greeting then back at her book, but then her head snapped back up and took a good look as Azuno smiled a big white toothy grin at her.

"I see you again today," he said leaning in her direction over the table.

"Uh huh." Rachael responded through the lump in her throat as she nervously bit her bottom lip and looked back down at her book. She had dreaded this unavoidable meeting. Rachael didn't want to believe her uneasiness could be the result of her parents' death or could there really be something to be worried about. Rachael waited for the tutor to sit down before she looked up again. Azuno looked busy solving equations so she turned her attention to the problem in Geometry she needed help with.

"May I listen, please?" Azuno asked the tutor when he started to explain the formula for the volume of an Isosceles Triangle. As the tutor described the triangle rules, how it could be used, and the importance of memorizing it, Azuno interrupted.

"Ahh, yes, we figure angle of roof to build for our round houses," He said, triumphant in his knowledge. He sounded smart to himself as he glanced at Rachael to see if she too had been impressed. He sensed she may be interested but he had difficulty reading her.

Before he could say anything else a quiet hissing voice warned him not to let her know too much of his village life or he may frighten her away. He sat back corrected and chose another Algebra equation to solve. Perplexed that he may have blown his cover, he devised what he may say next to send her off in another direction.

What other tribes used round houses? He silently entreated the Ancestors for the answer. The hissing voice told him to say Argentina, much further south from his home in Brazil. He would have to head for the library to study up on these people to be convincing.

"Are you Azuno?" The tutor asked, breaking into his thoughts. Although he didn't really need help, he turned the page to the longest equation and asked him how to solve for both X and Y. While the tutor explained the formulas that would help Azuno, Rachael stood and stowed her book in her backpack.

Azuno tried to think of any reason he could use to detain her, but nothing came so he chose to be patient and not scare her away with his zeal to get to know her. Everything depended on developing a relationship with her of trust to get her to go with him voluntarily. For how else would he get her across the many borders into Brazil? This may take longer than he anticipated. Lost in thought, he snapped out of it when he realized the tutor asked him the same question twice.

"Oh, excuse please," Azuno said feeling the heat of embarrassment rise on his olive skin.

"So, you like Rachael do ya?" The tutor chided. "Yeah, she's pretty for sure but not too bright when it comes to math. It seems to come natural to you though. How long have you been studying at Western?"

"First quarter in America," Azuno answered.

"You studied at the college level before you came here? You must have had good teachers for you to be doing so well," the tutor commented.

"No, natural to me. Same too as life if you pay attention. Lessons all there," Azuno replied. He, too, began to pack his books.

"Where do you come from then?"

"Way south," Azuno said over his shoulder as he smiled and thanked the tutor for his help. The student tutor shrugged his shoulders as he got up to help someone else.

Azuno went to the library and asked the counter person to help him find information on Argentina and the native people who lived there. He would not be caught off guard again. As the library assistant started toward the book stacks he needed, Azuno followed lost in thought about his finding her. Concern furrowed his eyebrows when he thought about the young man in the Math Lab. He seemed to be asking a lot of questions for someone who was supposed to be answering questions instead. What would be his interest? Azuno hoped he would not be an issue between him and Rachael. The last thing he needed complicating his mission, another obstacle.

CHAPTER 9

Rachael leaned against her dorm room door as the adrenaline from the flight through campus dissipated, the muscles in her neck and shoulders relaxed as she set down her heavy backpack.

Wow, how obvious can a person be? She thought to herself as she went over to the chair of her desk and sat down with a sigh.

That guy is definitely following me.

She jumped as her phone vibrated in her pocket. Scrambling to get the phone out before it went to voicemail she answered a bit out of breath.

"Aunt Jenny." She said with excitement raising her voice a bit too high. She flicked her long hair away from her ear and over her shoulder to hear her Aunt better.

"What? Sorry, I didn't hear that last sentence."

"I'm catching a flight to Alaska because Shelley's doctor told her she needed bed rest." Aunt Jenny repeated.

"Oh, she's alright isn't she, and the baby?" The worrisome news conjured up what Aunt Jenny told her about her mother, who had miscarried a baby late in her pregnancy. It flooded her heart with fear for her cousin.

"The baby seems fine for now, but the doctor has sent Shelley to bed for the next month," Aunt Jenny said. Relief replaced the panic.

"I'm flying up there to help them set up the nursery and to be there for the delivery. I don't know when I'll be back. What are your plans for Spring Break, honey?"

"I don't have any yet, I was thinking of coming home but maybe I will go with Lisa. Her family invited me to go on a ski trip to Whitefish in Montana. I haven't skied for a few years. I hope I remember how." Rachael planned as they talked.

"That would be fun, and it'll get you out of the city for a while. I really miss you sweetie," Aunt Jenny said as her voice cracked. Rachael's intuition told her it wasn't the reception that caused the pause in the conversation.

"Come visit me then. You can catch a flight to Seattle and I will pick you up and take you back after a couple of days to catch your flight to Alaska."

Quiet, then Aunt Jenny asked. "Don't you need to be studying for your finals?"

Rachael assured her she would be finished if she flew in on Thursday then Aunt Jenny could catch a flight Saturday out of SeaTac.

"I already checked the flights to Anchorage from Seattle. They leave several times a day. I really could delay a couple days to see you. I do miss you, honey." Aunt Jenny continued. "There's a flight at 8am, 12pm, 3:35, and 8pm. The 8 o'clock one is best I think. It lands at 9:15 so if you get here by 9:30 I think that would give me time enough to get to the pick-up area."

"Well, that settles it. Give my love to Uncle Ben and see you on Thursday night at 9:35 then. I can't wait." They both burst out laughing.

The two said their goodbyes and excitement replaced tears. Rachael couldn't wait to show Aunt Jenny around the campus.

Rachael made a mental note to talk to Lisa tomorrow if she ran into her. They didn't have any classes together this quarter which made it harder to spend time together. She would just have to call and catch up with her between classes. Right now, she must start cramming for finals.

Late into the night Rachael studied at her desk, struggling to keep her eyes open. A quiet voice startled her. It seemed to be coming from just outside the window on the other side of her desk. How could that be since she lived on the fourth floor and the only thing on the other side of the glass was air? Still puzzled, Rachael looked at the time. Two o'clock in the morning. Groggy, she stumbled to the door with a towel flung over her shoulder and her shower kit in her hand to brush her teeth and wash her face in the shared bathroom.

She reached for the door knob and heard a whisper.

"Rachael."

She spun around but no one was there. Her hand on the door knob shook as a shudder went through her.

"My dear, do not be frightened." Rachael heard the woman's voice louder than before. She turned toward the room and on the edge of her bed sat a beautiful woman in a long cotton dress smiling at her. She was a slight woman with the tiniest waist she had ever seen. The apparition held herself as if she were a queen. The severity of her hairstyle did not take away her beauty. She had it pulled back from her face in a tight bun at the nape of her neck, with small ringlets over her ears and temples, softening the severity of the hairstyle. Rachael stood frozen with one hand still on the door knob and the other squeezing the handle of her shower kit with her knuckles showing white through her skin.

"What...a.... who are you?" Rachael managed to get past the restriction of fear in her throat.

This is so unreal, I must be dreaming. She thought, trying to figure out how she should act.

"Just look at you, so beautiful. You do remind me of my own beautiful darling ladies when they were your age. As a matter of fact, my very own Rachel has eyes like yours. As blue as the Iowa sky," The woman replied with a soft English accent.

Rachael leaned against the door not trusting her knees to keep her upright.

"Elizabeth," she said in a whisper.

"Yes child, your Elizabeth," she whispered back with a twinkle in her eye, parroting Rachael in a teasing manner.

"How?" Rachael asked on the sigh that emptied her lungs and caused her to relax. A warm tingle vibrated throughout her body that proved she was awake, or did it? Undecided as to what to do, she stood, staring.

"Come, sit by me and we may learn of this wondrous meeting together," Elizabeth coaxed, patting the comforter next to where she sat.

Like an obedient child, Rachael responded to the beautiful compelling voice of her ancestor come to visit. Still in shock, she sat and stared at the figment of her imagination or dream or what, she could not tell.

Elizabeth giggled, and it sounded as beautiful as a bell. She reached up and touched Rachael's chin. "Close your mouth darling before you begin to catch flies."

Rachael laughed too, the light touch of Elizabeth's hand felt warm and real to her.

"You really are here, aren't you?" Rachael toughed Elizabeth's arm. Tears welled up in her eyes and Elizabeth took Rachael into her arms and rocked her.

"There. There, child." Elizabeth soothed her as she sobbed out all her loneliness. She smoothed Rachael's long golden hair and held her as she cried. "Yes, surely as real as you. Though I am not entirely sure myself how this all came about. No matter, I am here, and I do have a message for you." She gently sat Rachael up to look her in the eye. She reached into her sleeve and pulled out an embroidered handkerchief hidden there and wiped Rachael's cheeks dry.

"A message? From whom?" Rachael asked as she scrunched her eyebrows together.

"Dearest, you will cause lines on your brow if you do that too much." Elizabeth stroked Rachael's forehead until she relaxed her features.

"Whom do you think, my dear?" She said looking to the ceiling. Rachael studied Elizabeth for it seemed a long time before she realized the person she must be referring to was God himself.

"Your parents send their love," Elizabeth said as she adjusted a few stray strands of Rachael's hair behind her ear. Just like her mom used to do.

"They're with you? Well, of course they would be in heaven. They loved God even to death, I suppose, and you too. I have gotten so much closer to understanding God and my parents' decision to follow him by reading your journals. You know, your journals are helping me through this... horrible time without my parents. I'm so glad you are here. Wow, to finally really meet you, but I feel as though I already know you.

Wow.... Wow, I can't seem to stop my mouth." Rachael rambled on.

"We are quite alike, you and I." Elizabeth said with a great hug that filled Rachael with such warmth and joy she never wanted to leave her arms again.

"But to the message. This is very important, my dearest. Do you trust me that I would not steer you in the wrong direction?" Elizabeth looked deep into Rachael's eyes. "Well then, if you trust me I will tell you why I am here."

Rachael nodded then Elizabeth nodded in return.

"Azuno."

That one word dropped between them like a curtain. Rachael broke away and stood in disbelief. How could she know about that guy in the math lab? She must be dreaming.

"You said you would trust me. Now be good and listen to the rest, darling. You better sit down, for this is even more difficult to understand, and believe, than his name alone." Settling Rachael back down, she slid her arm around her waist.

"Dear darling child, I love you like you were my own dearest little Rachel. Azuno is your future. Can you trust me when I say to you to stop running away from him?"

"But, how? I don't even know him," Rachael questioned, this time without the rebellion rearing up inside. She tried to trust and believe but this seemed so unreal, so straight out of a weird creepy movie. And she had almost reassured herself.

"You will know him my dearest, only you must stay open and listen for the voice of God. He will send the Holy Spirit to direct your path. Do you know that voice? Sweet darling, the voice of God is calling you, loving you, guiding you. The voice is the Comforter that is with you all the days of your life."

"No, I don't know that voice." Rachael recalled a moment after her parents' funeral when peace flooded her, and she hadn't felt so alone.

"The comforter you said?"

"Yes."

"I did feel something like that, but I didn't hear a voice."

Elizabeth's smile was radiant when she heard this from Rachael.

"Praise be to our good Lord Almighty. You do have the Holy Spirit, only you are so unsure of yourself you did not recognize Him for who He is." Elizabeth hugged Rachael again.

"That is a start." She continued to teach Rachael about the Holy Spirit of God and what He was calling her to do.

"As your walk with God deepens and you understand more, the Voice of God will become clearer to you. Now, I must talk to you about Azuno. This is too exciting for words." Elizabeth broke out in a spontaneous rejoicing with her hands raised to the heavens then turned back to

Rachael as if she just remembered what she came to say.

"Azuno is your future, my child. Without him you will never find the healing you need. Go with him. Go with him." Elizabeth repeated with both hands holding Rachael away from her by her shoulders, looking deep into her eyes.

"Go with him for God has sent you for him. He is your future." Elizabeth hugged Rachael one more time then she vanished.

Rachael called her name, as she bolted upright from the open book on her desk she had been studying, but Elizabeth had disappeared. It must have been a dream. The creases on her face she could see on her face in the dark window acted like a mirror.

Though a dream, the message planted in her heart. Though alone now, Rachael did not feel alone. For the first time since her parents' death she did not feel alone. She imagined that the loneliness will never be a part of her again now that she had experienced something so extraordinary.

Beyond a doubt, someone had been looking out for her just beyond her own world. Rachael pushed her chair away from the desk and with wobbly legs walked over to her bed. She lay back with her arms around her shoulders where she remembered Elizabeth's last touch. She stared at the ceiling and ran through all that had happened in such a brief visit.

"Wow, what a trip." Rachael said, confused,

then laughed out loud. Her heart beat faster as she unraveled the mystery of Elizabeth's words. Shaking her head at the whirlwind of thoughts about Azuno and how he could be her future, Rachael pulled herself back up from the bed, grabbed her bathroom kit and towel from the hook next to the door and headed down the hall to brush her teeth before she went to bed. She had her final in Geometry this afternoon and must get some sleep.

As she crawled under her comforter it still seemed warm where Elizabeth had sat. As she snuggled down and curled her arms around a pillow, she slipped back into sleep with a long peaceful sigh.

CHAPTER 10

Rachael turned the corner into the Math Lab an hour before her final to get some last-minute encouragement and bumped into Azuno coming out.

"Oh. Sorry," she said with a smile as Azuno grabbed her shoulders to keep her from falling backward. Rachael noticed he didn't let go right away, and despite her late-night visitor, she fought against a slight resistance inside. She remembered Elizabeth's words and they echoed in her mind.

He is your future.

Azuno smiled back and watched Rachael's cheeks turn a pretty shade of pink as she looked up at him. His breath caught in his chest as the closeness gave him a startling view of her eyes, a deep blue with a slight green ring that circled the ink black pupils. Fear of those eyes climbed through his blood like the snuff his father used to conjure the spirits. Fear of losing himself in those eyes he remembered from the dream that started this remarkable trek across two continents in search of her. And now, standing so close he could bend his head slightly and touch her open lips with his. The idea startled him. He shuddered as his hands dropped away from her shoulders.

This woman is more powerful than I first imagined. I must keep my head. One look into her eyes, and she has put me in a trance. Shaking his head to clear it of the unsettling thoughts he stepped away from her.

He could not let her overpower him or he would lose all understanding. Azuno resolved to complete what he started out to do. He would not lose face with his people or give up his responsibility to become their leader or he would be lost to the Ancestors for all eternity. He would forever wander the spirit world, alone and forsaken. Azuno could not let that happen. He had a lot riding on this mission. He frowned and closed off any expression that might be read in his eyes. He did not want Rachael to read his thoughts.

He stepped around her to leave without a word.

"Azuno, wait." she said and reached out to touch his arm.

Azuno tried to decipher her expression, maybe pleading. No, this cannot be.

Where she touched him, he felt the warmth of her fingers as if his skin was seared by a hot iron, but he curbed the impulse to suck in his breath.

Confused by the sudden change in her actions, he turned to study her. She had avoided him all this time and finally she wanted to talk?

"Yes, what is it?" he asked.

"I...a...what are you doing this afternoon? I mean do you want to hang out?" Rachael asked, again the pink returned to her cheeks.

Hang what out? Azuno had no idea what she meant and waited for her to explain.

"Oh... hang out means sitting together and talking." The confusion cleared as he smiled and nodded his head in understanding of the teen-age slang she used but still suspicious as to her motive. He smiled his beguiling toothy smile to appease any fear in her. He found it a bit disconcerting that it seemed she had fallen into the Ancestors trap. Maybe this wouldn't be as difficult as he had first anticipated.

"Where to .... hang out?" Azuno asked with a bit of satisfaction.

"Well, could you meet me in the cafeteria after my Geometry final, around two?"

Azuno looked at the clock on the wall above the entrance where they stood. It was nearly noon; he had to suppress his feelings of luck that she initiated this contact.

"I will be there," he said with a nod and smiled another white broad grin.

"Good, I, I will see you at two," Rachael stammered over her shoulder as she turned toward the counter of the Math Lab.

Only for a moment did Azuno allow himself to watch her walk away. She was short but shaped like no other woman he had ever seen. She seemed fragile, like a spun glass figurine, like the ones he saw being formed outside the Imaginarium Gift shop on the east side of Boa Vista. A stabbing pain shot white hot through his head behind his eyes as he tore himself away from the sight of Rachael at the counter and forced himself out the door. The pain reminded him of the cost if he did not succeed. He must exchange her life for his; the Ancestors were clear on that point.

"She is the enemy, do not forget that." A hissing voice deep in the recesses of his mind reminded Azuno as the pain worsened to the point that he dropped onto a bench outside the Math building. He covered his eyes with the palms of his hands, pushing the pain back.

"I will not let you down," he whispered, and the pain lessened then left him.

He did not have much time; the Ancestors had increased their demands and urgency. But he still did not know how he planned to get Rachael to his father for he must convince her to go willingly or he would not be able to get her across the borders or on a plane with him for that matter.

He had but two hours to devise a plan. Azuno shot from the bench and raced to the cafeteria. He found a quiet corner on the second floor to be alone and paced back and forth raking his hands through his straight black hair cut short the way the other boys wore theirs on campus. Azuno caught his reflection in a window, he looked like a stranger. The men in his tribe wore their hair long in the back and cut just above the eyes.

He shook his head trying to block out unnecessary thoughts, so he could concentrate. Azuno made another circuit around the room, still with no more clarity. A growl of frustration began deep in his chest and he moved into the corner of the room, to avoid distracting the students trying to study.

Slowly, a small seed of an idea began to form in his mind. He smiled to himself as the idea became clear.

Of course, so simple. So simple in fact it might work.

Azuno looked at the clock across the room and decided to wait downstairs, not to miss Rachael when she came in. Skipping every other step Azuno sprang down the stairs with renewed hope that the ordeal would soon be over. This plan would not fail the Ancestors.

As he landed with a slight skid at the bottom of the stairs, he spotted Rachael across the large open room coming through the door. He waved and other students looked up. He smiled at them and pointed at Rachael, embarrassed.

You must be at your most convincing and charming or you will ruin our plans Azuno. The hissing voice inside his head reminded him with a stab of pain behind his left eye that made his lid shut involuntarily in a wink.

Walking up to Azuno at that moment, Rachael broke out in a laugh that sounded like music to his ears, as she winked back at him.

"What was that for?" She asked him as he reached for her backpack, sliding it off her shoulder, pouring on the charm. He guided her back up the stairs he just came down.

"I am not sure, something in my eye." He said as he rubbed it.

This part of the cafeteria had comfortable over stuffed couches and matching chairs. Bunches of large live trees, and ferns separated each furniture setting, all cozy under a roof of windows that looked up into a vast blue sky with wispy clouds floating past. It reminded him of his beloved jungle.

Azuno stopped at a couch with a coffee table in front of it and dropped her backpack onto it next to his. He offered Rachael a seat on the couch and chose the chair opposite, not too eager to be close to her.

He stared at her not knowing what to say. Silence stretched.

"So" Rachael said, then more silence and they both laughed which broke the ice.

"How was Geometry final?" Azuno asked. He had no idea what he needed to say to convince her to leave for South America with him over spring break.

"Fine, I hope. I'm just relieved it's over." She

said, and a heavy sigh escaped her as she relaxed against the corner of the couch.

"Do you have plans for break? I have to go back to my country for my father needs me to take care of some things with my new smartness," he said, quite proud of himself.

Rachael laughed again.

"Where is your home, Azuno?" She asked.

"Argentina...." He lied and watched for her reaction to see if she noticed. He did not have a lot of experience lying for no one lied in his tribe. No one lied for they feared that the Ancestors would know, and his people did not want the punishment they would administer. But now, they were the ones feeding him the lies to convince Rachael to go with him.

"In South America...." Rachael whispered, and she started to shake.

Go with him, a small voice urged her in her head.

"No," she said out loud.

"What, no? Yes. I do live in South America. That is my home, you doubt me?"

"Oh, no Azuno. I'm sorry, you misunderstood me. I was thinking of something else." Rachael explained as she put a hand over her pained and racing heart. "My parents.... they... died... in South America," she said as tears welled in the corners of her eyes. She was drawn into that world from her dream where she watched her parents die. Surprised by this display in front of a stranger, she wiped the tears with her sleeve and smiled at Azuno, hoping he wouldn't be uncomfortable with her emotions. Rachael noticed that darkness in his eyes again, but she believed it must have been because of her sadness about her parents.

More than discomfort plagued Azuno at that moment. The screaming in his head escalated so loud he barely could hear her quiet admission to him.

"Do you have plans?" Azuno tried again, desperate to quell the arguments going on in his head.

"Oh, I haven't decided yet. I was thinking on going skiing with a friend, but I haven't been able to arrange it with her and her family."

"Come with me to my family," he said staring deep into her eyes. He waited without making a move, not even breathing.

"Yes" Rachael said. Then her eyes opened wide. "No! I can't. Yes. Oh, I don't know."

"What will you do, Rachael? Stay.... Go? What?" Azuno asked not even imagining, not even wanting to believe she would come with him so easily. He waited for her reply with his heart beating a wild cadence in his chest.

◆ ◆ ◆

Rachael sat staring into the room.

I'm so confused. I want to listen to the voice, is it really God's spirit? That's what Elizabeth said but this terrifies me.

I don't know Azuno at all, what in the world am I thinking? Flying to Argentina with him is insane.

How can I even begin to contemplate such a thing and with a total stranger? How could I even begin to think about listening to a dream from some- one like Elizabeth, she's dead? What am I thinking, how could I possibly obey this voice in my head? She started gulping large breaths as panic began to close off her throat.

◆ ◆ ◆

With one fluid movement Azuno got out of the chair and slid onto the couch next to Rachael. He reached for her in fear that she would run away from him and he would never see her again. He touched her arm gently to not frighten her away. When she did not resist he pulled her into his arms and held her, speaking soothing words to her in his own language until she relaxed and pushed him away.

"I'm fine. Really. I don't know what came over me. I guess it was talking about my parents. I miss them so terribly. Sometimes it sneaks up on me and the pain of losing them is overwhelming.

I'm sorry, Azuno." Rachael turned away from him as if she needed privacy to pull herself together.

"Not to worry, Rachael. I am sorry to remind you of this great pain." Azuno meant it as he remembered the hut where her parents slept and died by his hand. A hint of regret hit him as he glanced at her with her head bowed away from his searching eyes. Then another pain pierced in his mind. The pain inflicted by the Ancestors as the punishment for caring that Rachael continued to grieve because of him.

What would she do if she knew it was I that caused this pain? Azuno turned away from Rachael in shame.

"I'll go with you Azuno," Rachael whispered as she looked over to him, his head hung, and his shoulders slumped over with what seemed like a great weight he carried there.
"I'll go with you to Argentina over spring break." She said firmer as his head lifted. Rachael watched the changing emotions cross over his face. A look like remorse clouded his face but quickly turned into triumph after she told him she would go with him.

That big, wide, white familiar grin she started to look forward to crept across his face. "We will have great fun, you and me." He said.
This is the right choice, beloved.

A peace flooded through her, and the fear was gone.

Now she had to figure out how to tell Aunt Jenny she planned to fly to South America with a total stranger for a week and not to worry?

Oh, Aunty, don't worry. Some dead lady in a dream told me to go with this guy to the bottom of the world where no one knows me and that I am going to be perfectly safe. That will work? I think I have completely lost my mind and I should march on down to the psych ward and commit myself, that's what I think.

Rachael laughed out loud and Azuno raised his eyebrow at her strange actions.

"Don't worry; I was just imagining telling my Aunt who is flying in tonight for a visit that I am going with you over spring break." Rachael explained, and she scrunched up her forehead.

Remember what I told you about that, Rachael, you will cause those wrinkles to stay on your forehead forever. She heard Elizabeth's musical voice reprimanding her.

This is insane.

Rachael shrugged her shoulders to alleviate tension she had been carrying there all day, and they began to make their plans. She decided not to worry her Aunt. She would not tell her. She would be too busy taking care of Shelley and the new baby to worry. Before she knew where she went, Rachael would be back safe and sound. Then she would tell Aunt Jenny of her adventure.

A leap of faith, my love, trust in the creator. Rachael tilted her head and closed her eyes to gauge what this quiet voice meant by that.

They planned to get plane tickets that left from the airport just after Aunt Jenny flew out for Alaska. Azuno agreed to meet her after she said good bye to her Aunt then they would get on their own plane heading south. Azuno told Rachael he already had his ticket and that it wouldn't be difficult to add another and change the flight time. He would make all the arrangements.

CHAPTER 11

Rachael went to her room to grab a jacket and throw a burrito in the microwave. She had just enough time to drive to Seattle to pick up Aunt Jenny. While she drove the hour and a half to the airport she planned her trip.

In the morning she'd call Roger and ask him to wire some money to her account in Bellingham, and then find her passport. She thought it must be in the file cabinet with her important papers at home. She couldn't ask Roger to get it for her; he would ask too many questions and alert Aunt Jenny.

Then, she remembered she had taken her passport and other important papers with her back to school and hid them between Elizabeth's journals. A sigh of relief escaped her, and she relaxed for the first time since she decided to do this crazy thing. Almost as if it had been meant to be. How else could she explain her impulse to grab her passport before she left home last December when she hadn't used it for three years? Could all this be working out because she had Elizabeth looking out for her? This must be Gods will then.

When she finally saw Aunt Jenny coming down the escalator from the plane at SeaTac, she squealed like a child and ran to her. Rachael looked forward to her visit, but she will have to evade any questions as to her plans for spring break and probably lie to her Aunt. That would be hard, but she convinced herself it was for Aunt Jenny's own good that she keep this trip a secret. She even wondered if she should tell her anything at all about Azuno or her visitation from Elizabeth.

She decided to tell her only the parts about meeting Azuno and that Elizabeth came to her in a dream but not until they got back to the dorm. She wanted to have plenty of time to explain her fears away. Aunt Jenny would not worry about the vivid dreams Rachael had, she seemed to have a logical explanation for every one of them.

Rachael would feel better when Aunt Jenny knew some of what she would be doing, though not quite sure why. How could Aunt Jenny believing a lie make her feel better? She shook the feeling of dread off, she hated to lie to anyone, especially someone she loved. She buried a thought that she would be relieved when these next two days were over.

As she and Aunt Jenny drove back to Rachael's dorm where they would share her tight quarters with a roll away cot, Aunt Jenny filled her in on everyone's health especially Shelley's.

"She is going stir-crazy lying in bed all the

time. You know Shelley. She's usually working on some kind of project or another and running around all the time. It's a good thing I'm going up there or she'd ignore the doctor's instructions. She's so worried that the nursery won't be ready in time. Someone needs to be there making sure she doesn't hurt herself or the baby. Did I tell you it was a boy?" Aunt Jenny took in a large breath.

"Winded much?" Rachael suppressed a chuckle.

"Oh, Rachael, I have done nothing but rattle on since I got in the car. Now tell me about you. How do you think your finals went?"

Rachael shrugged her shoulders and kept her eyes on the road. Time to lie to her. She had a good excuse not to look at her, she must pay attention to the Seattle traffic.

"I made plans with Lisa's family to go skiing in Montana with her. They are meeting me at the airport after I see you off Saturday afternoon," Rachael said with a cheerful note in her voice. She hoped her aunt would not notice how shallow it sounded in her ears.

"Are you nervous about the trip?" Aunt Jenny asked, turning in her seat to study Rachael with her head tilted to the side.

She noticed. Rachael knew that look anywhere, the two sisters had that one down pat.

"Yeah, a little." She lied again to cover the first. "I just haven't met her parents and spending a week with strangers has always been difficult for me. You know how I am kind of a loner."

Aunt Jenny began her encouraging lecture mode that reminded Rachael again of her mother. It made it more difficult to handle the guilt she felt creeping up her spine and settled between her shoulder blades. Despite the guilt, Rachael sighed with relief for her spin of a believable lie worked and now she had a reason to be packed and ready to go to the airport on Saturday. It bugged her though, it was too easy to lie.

Rachael listened to Aunt Jenny the rest of the drive and agreed with her that she really needed to get out more and make new friends. It seemed that she spent most of her time with her nose in the books. She encouraged Rachael to step out of her comfort zone and embrace life a little. She and Aunt Jenny had several of these conversations since the funeral about how difficult it had been for Rachael to trust people and allow others in.

She succeeded in that goal by letting Azuno in. This made her think of the last time she saw Azuno, how he had held her, comforted her in his strange native language. Startled a bit by the idea he no longer frightened her now that she was getting to know him, she smiled. She almost couldn't wait to tell Aunt Jenny about him.

"I know it was hard to get a word in edgewise with me doing all the talking but you seem different. Is everything ok with you?" Aunt Jenny said as they were lifting luggage out of Rachael's pearl white Subaru Sport in the parking lot next to her dorm building.

"There is so much I want to tell you I am not sure which wonderful thing I should start with. It's a very long story so I have been saving it for later. You know pajama talk like when we first discovered Elizabeth." Rachael hedged for more time to figure out exactly what to say but knew she would have to start talking as soon as the door shut behind them since Aunt Jenny couldn't wait to hear a marvelous story.

"Okay," Rachael laughed. Once they got to her room and Aunt Jenny came through the door and plopped onto the bed. She cupped her chin in her hands like she was not going to move until Rachael spilled the news. She decided to start at the beginning.

"Well, you know I told you about this guy that creeped me out?"

"Okay, yeah. You were worried that you were having prejudice issues." Aunt Jenny confirmed.

"You won't believe this but…. now, please promise me you won't think I'm crazy and feel I need to see a counselor… Promise?"

The look in Aunt Jenny's wide-open eyes held a mixture of fear and pleading. Rachael couldn't keep her in suspense any longer.

"I promise only if you can convince me that you're okay." Aunt Jenny answered with a tinge of suspicion in her voice.

"Fair enough. Well, Elizabeth came to me in a dream. It was so awesome, Aunt Jenny. I felt her, and she was warm, like she was a living breathing person sitting right there where you are sitting now. She had on an old-time dress with a high neckline and tiny waist. She was so beautiful and looked a little like me.

She told me stuff that no one else could have known like her Rachael having blue eyes just like mine. You know the daughter she had that died when she was six? Isn't that crazy?" Rachael took a breath and glanced at her Aunt to see how she took the quickly spat out revelation. Aunt Jenny just sat there, watching and assessing.

"There's more. She told me not to be afraid of Azuno." Now, Rachael hesitated because she didn't want to tell her that Elizabeth told her to go with him. "She said he was my future. Can you believe it? And I have been running away from him from the first day I met him because of the color of his skin. Okay, now you can tell me I am insane and call the wagon to take me to the funny farm," Rachael laughed trying to lighten the look on Aunt Jenny's face.

Her Aunt sat for a few seconds with a glazed look on her face. Worry and guilt now played tug-of-war with Rachael's neck muscles.

"So, you met this guy that creeped you out, then you had a dream that Elizabeth came to you and she was real. Then she told you to go after this guy that creeped you out and you did?"

"Yeah, kind of, and he is really.... I don't know.... nice, cool, well maybe not cool because he doesn't even know what the word means. It was funny when I asked him to hang out with me and his face was blank.... He wasn't sure what I meant because he is from Argentina."

Let's see if that doesn't open a can of worms.

Aunt Jenny's eyes shot open wide and she sat up straight as if now she really needed to pay attention to what Rachael said.

"Argentina is in South America, Rachael." Aunt Jenny closed her eyes. Rachael noticed her aunt's face pale and sat beside her. Putting her arm around her she hugged her close.

"Aunty don't worry so much. It will be fine. I will be careful getting to know him and spend a lot of time with him. Besides Argentina is clear at the bottom of South America and not anywhere near where Mom and Dad were. Please trust me. And you know Elizabeth, she is a no-nonsense woman, and would she steer me wrong?"

"I insist on meeting this Azuno person." Rachael agreed to take her to the cafeteria the next morning for breakfast to see if they could find him.

"What? You don't text?" Aunt Jenny asked.

"Like I said Aunty, we are taking it slow."

CHAPTER 12

O nce Rachael and Aunt Jenny settled into the dorm room it was past midnight.

"Take my bed Auntie; it'll be better for you. Besides, after Shelley's baby's born you won't be getting much sleep."

Aunt Jenny crawled into the crisp cotton sheets on Rachael's bed and they settled in for a night of catching up.

Despite being tired, they talked late. Aunt Jenny wanted to know more about Azuno, but she knew she wouldn't get anywhere if she pushed. She tried several different approaches in her head before she said anything out loud. Just as she opened her mouth to ask the question she thought the least pushy, a quiet voice in her head spoke and stopped her words.

Will you trust me, Jenny?

Jesus' soft searching question brought tears to her eyes. How could she answer that? She sensed Jesus asking her to let her young niece decide something for herself.

But she is so young, Lord, and she doesn't know what she's doing. She has no parents, so someone needs to be looking out for her.

Will you trust me? Jesus asked her again.

Could she do that? Let her go; get out of God's way? Rachael must make a stand for Jesus in her own time. Aunt Jenny's heart broke all over again; just as it did when she watched Rachael standing over the open grave of her parents.

Let her go? She must obey. She clamped her mouth closed and would not interfere despite her need to parent Rachael. Aunt Jenny reached over to the bedside stand and turned off the lamp.

"Sweet dreams, honey," Aunt Jenny said with a sigh.

"Good night Auntie, I love you." Rachael bounced around on the squeaky cot until she got comfortable.

"Love you too, more than you know." She tried to put a smile on her face, so Rachael could hear it in her voice in the dark. Jenny did not want to alert Rachael to the turmoil in her heart. Something was about to happen, and it was going to be hard for her to stay out of it.

"Aunt Jenny? Everything will be alright, you'll see."

Surprisingly, it brought little comfort.

"I am sure you're right. Forgive me for being so parental. I guess it's my way of making up for not having your mom to keep you safe so that you don't get hurt again." Aunt Jenny smiled in the dark. "But God sometimes has to remind me of just who is in control." Turning on her side and looking down at Rachael, she could see her wide eyes staring up at her from the light leaking through the slats in the blinds on the window.

"What do you mean, in control? Does God control everything, does he know my thoughts, and what I say or do?"

"Well, he controls the universe and keeps all the planets in place. He controls the supernatural things of this world, but he will not control his created beings. Only if you ask him to will he control your life. But he's not like a drill sergeant, more like a loving Father with his toddler."

"Why would I want to let him control my life? I'm doing fine without him, aren't I?" Rachael asked, her tone of voice sounded confused and maybe a bit troubled.

"Let me explain it better: If a toddler is crawling toward a blazing fire in a woodstove and could get burned, a good father would try to redirect him, give him other options.

"God wants to protect you from the things that could burn you or separate you from him like sin or heading down the wrong road away from him, and toward something that you may think will bring you happiness, but he knows it won't."

It was silent in the dark room. Aunt Jenny waited for Rachael to think about what she had said but feared she went too far. She hoped she hadn't pushed Rachael away or confused her more.

"Does that make any sense, or answer your question?"

"Yeah, I guess so but I'm still hung up on the created beings thing you said. Who are created beings, just people right?" Rachael pushed up on her elbow and rested her head in her hand waiting for Aunt Jenny's answer.

"Not entirely, God created mankind, starting with Adam and Eve, along with all the creatures of the earth. He also created the angels. We have the freedom to choose to love God. He created us so that we would voluntarily love him and not be like robots. We choose to love those around us or not love them; how much sweeter is a love that is given freely by me to you than if I was obligated or commanded to love you. It is that much sweeter when love is given back. More than sweet if the love is between you and an almighty God who can offer so much more than what there is here on earth; Eternal life with him in heaven when you get there." Aunt Jenny took a breath.

"Wow, you could be a preacher, Auntie." Rachael said smiling. "So, I have to choose to love God in order for him to love me?"

"Nope, he already loved you before you were even born. There is a scripture I think it's in Psalms somewhere that says 'He loved me before he knit me in my mother's womb' or something like that."

"But, if that's true then where is my choice? If he knows all the things I will do even before I do them then how do I choose my own path? And for that matter then why do we exist, what's our purpose? I mean, what's the point of choice if he already knows everything, whether we will choose him or not choose him?" Rachael let out a frustrated sigh.

"Does the father of a toddler know his son will become a doctor when he grows up? No, but he will do his best to guide and direct his path in that direction if his child shows interest in medicine. Our purpose, as we were designed, is to live our lives according to his will in obedience to him and he would be our heavenly father. He wanted to be a father and he had the capacity to create us, so he did."

Rachael got up out of bed and paced the room. Aunt Jenny waited for a few minutes for Rachael to process.

"God will guide you if you ask him to and really listen to him, but you have to learn to listen for his voice and know it's the voice of God who is talking to you."

Rachael stopped in her tracks and spun around to face Aunt Jenny.

"That's what Elizabeth said, listen for God's voice. How will I know it's him and not just my own imagination?" Rachael resumed her pacing. "I thought I heard a voice before and now I'm getting visits from dead relatives."

"That's a good question." Aunt Jenny suppressed a chuckle with difficulty. "Getting to know God from the bible will help you learn his voice from those of the adversary, Satan and his demons." Aunt Jenny sat up on her bunk and crossed her legs. She knew this would keep them up for some time, now that she broached the subject of the dark world of fallen angels.

Rachael sat on the cot and faced her Aunt. "You believe in Satan and demons? My Psych professor told us that people made Satan and demons up to scare little children into obedience, that there's no such things in this world. Hard to know what to believe."   "Do you believe in angels, Rachael?" Aunt Jenny asked and waited for her niece to process the question.

"Well, Angels are all through the bible, aren't they?"

Aunt Jenny nodded.

"Okay, then yes I do believe in angels."

"Okay, then you must also believe in demons because they're angels that have chosen to rebel against God. Let me go back to the beginning. God created an angel he named Lucifer. He was the most beautiful angel of them all and because of that, many of the other angels looked up to him. He excelled in everything, and God was proud of him, so much so that he set him up to be in command of other angels.

"Well, that caused a chain of events which to this day produces wars. Lucifer thought that he should be above God. And that's what instigated his downfall, him and a third of the angels which followed him. Now he is called Satan and Devil as well as other names that depict his evil, corrupted heart.

"As active as angels are in the supernatural world, here they're behind a veil God has put between us and them or we would be scared to death, so are the demons that roam the earth invisible to our physical eyes: Invisible but no less as real as the angels that fight the demons for our protection and for our souls.

"You want to know what camp you are in at all times. You want to know you are in God's camp where you are loved. That doesn't mean all good things will happen to you, it just means that if something should happen to you then you know you will be in the arms of Jesus when you leave this world...." A feeling of dread flooded through Aunt Jenny's veins, her hands became clammy and cold.

Is that what you are asking me to do God? No, dear Lord, don't take Rachael too. Not yet, I'm not ready for that. I can't.

Trust me Jenny, will you trust me?

Peace washed over Aunt Jenny and the dread left. Peace from the comforter as a gift from God so that Jenny would not suffer from fear. He wanted Jenny to have faith.

"How do I know what camp I am in? I want to be in God's camp since you, my parents, and even Elizabeth were sure that God's camp is the right one to be in. What do I do to get there?" Putting her fears aside, Aunt Jenny got up and sat with Rachael. She put her arm around her niece's young shoulders and hugged her with tears flowing down her cheeks, dripping off her chin.

"I am so happy for you. Do you really want Jesus as your savior?"

"Jesus, yes, I want him to be my camp counselor so to speak, right?"

Jenny laughed.

"Okay, sort of right. Jesus is God's son who was sent to earth to live as a man and be sinless.... I'll tell you that long story later. Anyway, he chose to die for all of us and take on our sins that separate us from a relationship with God. He died in your place so that you may have the opportunity to live with him and God in heaven. He paid your ransom from sin in a way so that you would be set free to love and worship his father openly, to become one of his children, like the father with the toddler."

"Oh, I'm beginning to get it. So, what do I have to do to join this camp?"

"Ask God to forgive you of any sins you have committed knowingly and unknowingly. Ask God to come into your life and be your God, to guide you and send his holy spirit to teach and direct your path. Tell him you believe that Jesus is his son and that he died for you so that you might live with him every day. Then thank Jesus for purchasing you from sin's death. And then say Amen." Aunt Jenny said as she held both of Rachael's hands in her own.

"That's it, and then I'm free?"

"Well, yes and no. You will want to get to know who God is by reading his word and then as you grow, like a toddler grows, into an adult you will begin to recognize the paths he has mapped out for you. You will get to know his voice, as well as you recognize mine."

"I do want that more than anything, Aunt Jenny." Rachael said as she threw her arms around her aunt and they laughed in complete joy. They bowed their heads and held hands. Aunt Jenny spoke the sinner's prayer and Rachael repeated it. Tears began to flow down Rachael's face. When they were done and the tears wiped away with the sleeves of their pajamas it was past two in the morning.

Aunt Jenny pulled herself off the low cot and tucked Rachael in, kissing her on both cheeks and on her forehead. Aunt Jenny crawled into her own bed, adjusted her pillow and pulled the comforter over her; all was quiet except for Rachael's breathing, she had already dropped into a deep sleep.

CHAPTER 13

After Rachael left the cafeteria to pick her aunt up at the airport, Azuno pulled his cell phone from his pocket and pressed the call button for the first number he had on his speed dial list.

"It is done.... She agreed.... Change flight time to Saturday afternoon. You know what to do." Azuno snapped the phone shut and stared off into the distance. There was a coldness to him that he had never noticed before. Almost as if Azuno no longer existed. No emotion. Like the other time, when he crept through the jungle to kill Rachael's parents. He had worried about getting to know their child, how watching her grieve would affect him, but his heart had turned to stone.

He went over the events of the past hour as he walked to his apartment and contemplated how simple it had been to convince her to go with him to South America. He sensed that Rachael had no idea what would become of her and the turnaround must have been supernatural. If the Ancestors had this much power, then why did they not eliminate her themselves, without his help? There must be some limit or barrier to their power. Why go through all this trouble to take her out of the country and to his home to remove her from the living?

Azuno guessed it had something to do with the distance away from the Ancestor's power, away from their origins. Or, could it be that his father needed to use her death as an example to anyone who may challenge him or the Ancestors? He shook his head and forced himself not to think about it.

Once he reached his room, the exhaustion overcame him. He had not slept much these past few days. Without even eating dinner he slid down to his sleeping mat.

He slept so deep that he did not stir for twelve hours and woke up in the same position he fell asleep in. He had fallen asleep before the sun set the night before. Now, he waited for the sun to rise on a new day.

His stomach growled. Azuno rubbed the ache in his gut while he fixed himself some hot polenta and milk with honey drizzled over the steaming cereal. He sat at his dinette table gazing out the window facing east and waited. The first rays of a beautiful spring morning stretched out over the Cascade Mountains, and he began to plan his day.

He still had one final to finish then winter quarter would be over for him. He imagined himself coming back here to complete his studies once he accomplished his mission.

It will seem strange to be here without Rachael for I came to America only for her. Now it will be different. Will I be allowed to come back? Will Father let me go, even if it would be for the benefit of our people?

Azuno did not think so. His father would not see it that way. He would only see that the threat had been eliminated, and all could go back to the way it was. But Azuno had changed and he didn't think anything would be the same now that he had a taste of his own intelligence. He wanted to finish college.

He listed what he had accomplished in just a few months. He had learned a difficult language, he had set himself up in an apartment in a city and a country he had never been in before, succeeded in his first three classes of English, Algebra, and Science, found a job and kept it, and developed several relationships along the way to accomplish his goals, mostly with teachers. Now he saw these goals come to fruition, and it was almost anticlimactic. He recognized the extreme change compared to the scared boy that left his village a few months ago.

The sun peeked over the ridgeline and shined across his face. Azuno shut his eyes and imagined himself back in the Amazon basking in the sun on the hills where he grew up. If he imagined hard enough he could hear the toucans in the kapok trees that grew all throughout his beloved jungle. The jungle he would see again in only a few more days.

Azuno glanced at the clock, time for his Algebra final. Then he planned to "hang out" in the cafeteria to see if Rachael would show up to eat lunch. He wanted to make sure that his plans ran smooth and her Aunt would not cause any interference. He must charm Aunt Jenny and put her at ease.

Grabbing his backpack, he slung it over one shoulder and left for the college. He walked with long, quick strides through the streets near his apartment. The birds sang in the maple trees that were only beginning to leaf out along the street. Here and there in the sky white, bulky clouds skidded over the sun then passed, leaving the air warm, then cold, then warm again. He focused on these things to continue to have his mind all to himself. It seemed that today had less noise than usual.

Once he reached his class and took his seat, the bell rang. The teacher closed the door and passed the tests down each row, counting the students then the tests from the pile he balanced on his arm.

Azuno pulled out his calculator and a number 2 pencil, waiting for the student in front of him to pass the stack, swiveling in his seat he passed the rest behind him to the next student. It was a timed exam, Azuno checked the clock on the wall and realized that he would be doing a lot of clock watching for the next few days until he had Rachael on the plane to South America.

"Begin," the teacher said as he hit his stopwatch and headed to his desk.

Azuno flipped his test over and smiled at the simplicity of the questions. A quiet laugh echoed in his head. The malicious voice began screaming random numbers out trying to trip him up until beads of sweat popped out on Azuno's forehead. He concentrated to ignore the obnoxious voice.

Moving on to the next page his concentration became easier. He found that if he just ignored the voice it would go away. He blocked out everything but the equations. Algebra took just enough of his attention to allow him to escape into a different world; a world where only numbers could speak. Azuno raised his head in surprise at that thought. He would try this later when he wished for the Ancestors to not plague him the way they had these past few months.

As he turned to the third page, he glanced at the clock. At this rate he would be finished well before the class was out and heading to the cafeteria. His heart thumped hard in his chest, and he pushed the memory of Rachael cradled in his arms deep in the recesses of his mind to protect that thought from the attack he knew would come. One more page......

Azuno put his calculator and pencil away,

got up and shouldered his pack. Turning to the front of the room he took his test to the teacher. As he left he glanced over the classroom and several of the students looked at him with scrunched up faces. He finished first and that made him smile. Somehow, he would come back regardless of what his father wanted of him.

CHAPTER 14

There he is, Auntie, over there at that table by the window," Rachael said as she pointed toward the back of the cafeteria. Aunt Jenny turned to where Rachael directed, and a young man stood up when he saw her pointing at him. He looked just like all the other students except to Aunt Jenny he seemed a bit nervous shifting his weight to one foot then the other, as if he couldn't decide to stay or run.

This made Aunt Jenny want to giggle but she held it back. It did her heart good to see him so nervous to meet her, and she relaxed because of it. Any young man that nervous to meet the family of the girl he liked, seemed very normal to her. As they crossed the room, Azuno walked toward them and they met half way. Azuno reached his hand out and took Aunt Jenny's outstretched hand in both of his.

"It's so nice to meet you." They both said in unison and laughed together. This broke the possible tension between them. Aunt Jenny took a good look at him now from the top of his shiny black hair down to the neat khaki pants and button up, tucked in shirt, and tennis shoes. Then, their eyes met. What did Aunt Jenny see for a brief moment in his eyes? Fear?

Well, if he fears me he will treat my Rachael with respect. She thought.

"We came to eat lunch, have you eaten?" Aunt Jenny asked Azuno.

"No, I wait for you," Azuno answered with his white grin breaking across his face.

The three of them turned and headed to order food, Azuno guiding the ladies to walk before him. Aunt Jenny had Rachael go before her as she smiled back at Azuno, forming the many questions she planned to ask once they sat down.

After they paid for their food, Azuno suggested a table in the sunny second floor where he and Rachael liked to sit. He explained to Aunt Jenny the funny story of his first "hanging out" session as they chose a corner where they would have some privacy to get to know each other better.

"Rachael told me. I thought it was funny how, even though you seem to know the English language well, teenage slang is an entirely different thing all together. I guess now you can say that you are multilingual." And that made Rachael and Aunt Jenny laugh at Azuno's face as he tried to decipher the new strange word "multi-lingual".

Rachael leaned toward Azuno and said behind her hand "Multi means many and lingual means language." Azuno's face changed from scrunched up confusion to open understanding.

"Rachael told me you go to Alaska to help with new baby," Azuno said leaning toward Aunt Jenny.

"Yes, my son and his wife are expecting their first child. I am so excited to be there to see him come into this world." Aunt Jenny smiled.

"Him? How do you know this?" Confusion spread across his face again.

"Oh, they were able to see he was a boy when they did an ultrasound." She explained but still he didn't understand. Aunt Jenny described what happens when a woman has an ultrasound. She pulled the pictures out of her purse. Shelley sent them in the announcement before she left to visit Rachael and handed them to Azuno.

Turning the pictures this way then that way like he held the wheel of a car and driving around sharp corners, the comical look on his face made both the ladies struggle to hold back laughter. Rachael scooted closer to Azuno to look over his shoulder. Aunt Jenny came to stand behind them, pointing out parts of the baby in the black and white snapshot taken of the procedure.

"That's his head, and there are his eyes and lips. See, he is sucking his thumb. Now here are his feet and legs and there is his.... well... you can see he is a boy." Aunt Jenny's face reddened, and she sat back down. Now, it was Rachael and Azuno's turn to laugh at Aunt Jenny's discomfort.

"So...a...machine looks under the skin of a woman and can see the baby?" He asked still holding the picture with wide eyes, studying every shadow and dark spot as if still amazed.

"Yep, that's modern medicine. It really is amazing isn't it?" Aunt Jenny replied.

"Yes. A... a... ma.... zing," Azuno said trying out yet another unfamiliar word.

"So, Azuno, Rachael tells me you are from Argentina. Tell me what it's like."

The question surprised him. He had to think so he made a show of looking at the ultrasound photo again, repeated his new word 'amazing' and handed the picture back to Aunt Jenny. This gave him enough time to think of an answer, remembering the research he had done in the library just after he and Rachael had met.

"Like here only in Spanish and turned around... upside down? How to say? We now finish harvest.... and will perform celebration of good harvest and then for winter. This is good time to visit Argentina. Beautiful colors, beautiful music and dancing in the streets, beautiful people, beautiful food." He answered with only one discernable hesitation.

"What do you do there?"

"I do there?" He asked, not understanding if she asked what he did, or his fictitious people did there?

"Yes, you and your family. What does your

father do?"

"He is a…. doctor. He helps… people with simple things like sickness. He learned from his father but not go to school. That is why I come to school to better help people, more than my father." He answered, trying to veer the conversation away from his people and back onto him.

"Oh, that's nice. So, you want to become a doctor? Then what will you do, go back to Argentina and work with your father?"

This woman had many questions, Azuno knew it would be difficult but now beads of sweat began to tickle the hairs on the back of his neck.

You can do this, Azuno, you know what will happen if you don't.

The hissing voice reminded him that everything rode on convincing this one woman he was a good man.

"I am not sure what I will do yet," He answered honestly. He did not know so many things at this point. Azuno relaxed, comfortable that this truth would set well with Rachael's aunt. He did not know what tomorrow would bring, let alone a month or a year from now.

"Fair enough, it takes ten years to complete a medical degree. A lot can change in that much time." Aunt Jenny said patting his hands that were clasped together tight on the table in front of him. With her hand resting on his, he let out a sigh and they smiled at each other, breaking the awkward silence.

◆ ◆ ◆

As Aunt Jenny reached for her soda, her phone rang. They all jumped, still showing a bit of tension between them. She scrambled in her purse for the phone and answered just in time before it went to voicemail.

"Hi honey, is everything alright?" Aunt Jenny blurted out after she saw Sam's picture on the caller ID.

"Oh, thank God, Mom, you answered. It's Shelley, they've admitted her to the hospital and they're trying to stop her from delivering. Mom, you gotta come now." Sam blurted out as soon as she answered. Aunt Jenny could hear the tears of fear just under the surface of her son's voice.

"Take a breath sweetheart, do the doctors say she is doing okay?"

Jenny looked from Rachael to Azuno then back.

"Just come Mom, I need you."

"Okay. Well, I'll call you right back when I get an earlier flight. Tell Shelley everything will be okay. She's in good hands; the doctors will take care of her." Aunt Jenny reached for Rachael's hand and squeezed it tight trying to keep fear out of her voice.

"You better get back to her, honey. I will call you right back. Sam…. I'm praying, Bye." Aunt Jenny hit the end button on her phone and prayed.

"What?" Rachael asked, shaking her arm as she tugged on her sleeve.

"Shelley's in the hospital, she started bleeding. The baby seems fine, so they are just monitoring them both, waiting to see if they need to do an emergency C-section." She answered while she rummaged through her purse and brought out her plane ticket, searching for the number to call to change her flight.

Dialing the ticket counter, she entreated the Lord to be with her to make everything fall into place and to be with Shelley and baby.

As Aunt Jenny made the arrangements, Rachael reached toward Azuno and took his hand. She imagined the great loss they all would feel if something should happen to that baby so soon after her parent's funeral. This tiny blessing gave them hope. Rachael hung on every word that her aunt spoke to the person at the ticket counter.

"How soon can we get to the airport?" She asked, pulling the phone away from her ear.

Rachael calculated the time of day and whether I-5 would be clogged with commuters.

"Hour and a half, maybe more or less depending on traffic." Aunt Jenny looked at her watch as she conveyed this to the person on the other end of her phone.

"Okay.... okay.... Thank you so much. I will

be there as soon as I can. I am sure no later than three. Thank you again. Bye." Hanging up the phone and jumping to her feet Aunt Jenny reached out to Azuno taking both his hands as he and Rachael rose with her.

"We gotta go. It was so nice to meet you and I hope I get to see you again soon but we gotta go. Take care." Aunt Jenny grabbed Rachael by the hand and headed for the stairs.

"Will I see you when I get back?" Rachael asked over her shoulder.

"I will wait for you." Azuno called after them.

As the two women speed-walked through the cafeteria and out to the courtyard then raced to Rachael's dorm room Aunt Jenny dialed Sam back and filled him in on her flight time.

Rachael watch Aunt Jenny stuff her night-gown into her suitcase and race back out the door. She chased after her to the elevator. It had only been minutes since the call to the airport by the time they were in the car and speeding down I-5 toward Seattle and SeaTac airport. They made good time, the freeway miraculously clearer than normal for this time of day. Aunt Jenny said a prayer out loud for the safety of Shelley and the baby, as well as their safety and lack of police, so they wouldn't get caught for speeding.

As they pulled up to the loading station curb at the airport, a uniformed man took Aunt Jenny's luggage. He had tags ready for each piece.

"They are holding the plane Mam, please don't worry," The security officer explained as he attached the tags and put them on a motorized cart.

Aunt Jenny hugged Rachael good-bye then the cart whisked her away as the man skillfully beeped his horn and dodged through the people until they went around a corner.

Rachael looked over the crowded lobby of the airport, her heart filled with anxiety for her cousin and the new baby about to be born, yet she let out a sigh of relief. She wouldn't have to be careful she might slip up and say something about her trip to Argentina.

As she got into her car for the long drive back to school, she had some time to think about everything. She took the opportunity to try out this new prayer thing she and Aunt Jenny started the night before.

"Okay God, hi. I really don't know how to do this but here goes. I am worried about Shelley and the baby so could you be sure to take care of them? Thank you. And be with me on this trip with Azuno... I guess you already are since you were the one choreographing the whole thing. I think I would like to thank you for that too. He's... becoming someone important to me, whatever that means right now. I want to do the right thing so please be with me, help me know what to do, and help me understand and hear your voice. Thank you for my Aunt Jenny and bless her so much since she has been so good to me. Sorry for lying to her. I hope you understand why I did it. To do what Elizabeth told me to do and go with Azuno I knew Aunt Jenny would have been hurt and afraid for me if I told her the truth. Thank you, Jesus, for loving me. I love you. Amen.

CHAPTER 15

Azuno watched Rachael and her Aunt rush out of the cafeteria. As soon as they were out of sight, an explosion of voices went off in his head, screaming and fighting with each other. It took him great self-control to hold onto his sanity. He could not understand why they were angry at him. He had done his very best to make this trip happen and he had tried to assure them that they would get on that plane tomorrow. The Ancestors could count on it. So why war between themselves now, knocking around so noisily in his brain, causing him to get another headache?

He sat down and grabbed his Algebra book, took out a sheet of fresh notebook paper, opened the book to a part that the class hadn't covered and started working the equations. This would be his first experiment of controlling his own mind. He would silence the voices if it took him all day, as he waited for Rachael.

Find the product of n where...ENAMY...n equals seven...KILL HER... thirteen times y.... FAIL, AND YOU WILL DIE ......exponent of fifty-six is.... DEAD....DEAD...DEAD

The voices chanted on as he continued to ignore them until they started stabbing at his eyes from the inside of his skull.

"Stop."

He commanded them out loud with authority in his voice, and they quieted down but didn't quite stop. A new revelation to Azuno. Another tidbit of information he stored away for the future. He went back to his mathematical solutions and as he became engrossed in the systematic rhythm of the questions the voices receded into nothingness. Before Azuno realized, he had written out several pages of questions, and Rachael had plopped down on the couch beside him with an exhausted sigh.

"What a relief. Now, that Aunt Jenny is gone, we don't have to stress out about anything, well except for what I need to pack. You said it's fall now in Argentina so pretty much the same clothes I am wearing now, jeans and a sweater?" Rachael asked Azuno as he contemplated what she would need.

She will need nothing.

A flood of sadness washed over his heart when he heard this strange voice, a new voice, while he looked at her in the soft pink sweater she wore. Pink went well with her dark golden hair and blue eyes. He wanted to touch her and pull her into his arms, smell the clean fresh scent of her as he did the last time when he comforted her.

Pink goes well with red. Her blood will be flow-

ing soon and the power you will wield because of her will far exceed that of your father. Just think of what you will do for your people once you are in command.

Azuno had not heard this smooth, beguiling voice before, it entreated instead of threatened, and seemed to make more sense than the others. This voice wove a visual of him in his father's ceremonial robes but practicing real medicine. Medicine he will learn at the university.

"What's the matter? You're staring at me like.... I don't know, but you're giving me the creeps again," Rachael said pushing further back into the couch's cushioned arm rest.

Azuno shook his head, as if that would clear the disturbing vision.

"Ah.... I was thinking about the plane. Planes are.... frightful to me." Azuno sat back in the couch and grabbed the other armrest like he held on for dear life. He mimicked the pressure of the airplane taking off, pushing him back in his seat as he made a face like it pulled his skin back in a grimace, making a whooshing sound like a plane as it takes off. Rachael exploded in laughter.

Azuno laughed too, her laugh was infectious.

"You creeps still? What is creeps?" He asked leaning toward Rachael.

"Oh, maybe you don't want to know," She said. Azuno watched as the warmth of embarrassment slid up her face, she reached up to touch her cheeks then turned away.

"I do want to know. I want to know all things," He said, as he leaned closer to Rachael to give her his full attention.

"Well then, it is an expression of one feeling fearful or scared. Like something is crawling up your skin and making you shiver with fear." Rachael explained. "Please don't take it personally. It's just another teenage slang word, not really meant to be taken literal."

Azuno still did not understand.

"What is slang mean?" She used so many unfamiliar words. His people said what they meant and meant what they said, or they did not speak at all. A concept the people of America, he had met so far, did not understand. Everything seemed to be half-truths and pretend emotions.

For this reason, he would be glad to complete his schooling and go back to the Amazon where life was much simpler; however, because of his delicate mission this cultural difference worked to his advantage.

"Well, I had never thought about it, but I think it means words teenagers make up to express something that makes sense only to other teenagers. It kind of sounds cool or funny and gives us a voice or language all our own." Azuno smiled as he processed, nodding his head, as he tried to understand.

"I guess we had better get something to eat then go pack for our trip," Rachael said as she slowly got up and stretched her arms over her head. She closed her eyes and turned her face to the heavens and smiled.

Azuno stood in front of her, watching the expressions change on her face. Her pretty face and sweet smile mesmerized him.

"Hey, do you have a phone? Since we don't have to worry about Aunt Jenny, you can ride with me to the airport," She said as she took her cell phone out of her pocket and typed in the area code waiting for him to give her the rest of the number.

Azuno did not know the number to his phone. It was given to him by Kumata in Boa Vista. She was the one who made all the arrangements for their flight and keeping Shazundo informed of the plans, he imagined. He had not used the phone for any other purpose. He saw no need for Rachael to have the number. He could just meet her in the cafeteria at an agreed time.

"We meet here tomorrow, twelve, take lunch to airport. That good?" Azuno asked as he put a hand on each of Rachael's delicate shoulders and one of his thumbs lightly touched her skin at the base of her neck. He rested it there, thrilling to the beat of her heart through the vein he felt ba-bump just under her skin. Her warmth and life warred with his duty and the life of his people. Even though he wanted to choose her, he could not. He would lose too much. He dropped his hands with a pasted on smile he did not feel and grabbed up his back pack.

"Tomorrow at twelve." He turned to leave.

He looked over his shoulder and waved as Rachael turned to go out a different door.

CHAPTER 16

Rachael finished packing, she had very little in her suitcase to make the trip easier. She had her backpack and a small rolling case with a telescoping handle that would fit in the overhead storage. Both bags sat by the door waiting for morning. She had some time left after getting ready for bed and she grabbed the journal, a habit she had developed so she could feel closer to Elizabeth.

She leafed through the old pages to find where she left off. Rachael had been so busy studying for finals and had forgotten she had finished the first journal. Reaching deeper into the bottom drawer of her nightstand, she dragged out the next journal box. As she took off the ribbon she recalled the last entry she read, when the ship reached New Orleans and they all finally stood on dry ground again, much to the joyous relief of Elizabeth.

On the front of this journal Elizabeth wrote a title. "The Plains in Spring 1853– An Overland Journey to Zion". Rachael closed her eyes and imagined the Elizabeth she met carrying a newborn baby in her arms sitting on the seat of a covered wagon with her blue eyes sparkling under her sun bonnet. Rachael opened the journal and the first words jumped out at her as if she had been there, now that she knew each of the performers in this real-life play, especially Elizabeth herself.

May 6th, 1853

We are finally ready after six weeks of preparation for the trail. Charles and the boys have made fine purchases of a pair of strong oxen to pull the wagon and two healthy quarter horses, one male and one female, that we will breed once we get to our new home in Salt Lake City. The stallion is a bit headstrong, so Charles has taken charge of him while the two boys ride together on the mare so as not to have to ride in the wagon with the women.

When we arrived in Keokuk, Iowa it was a pleasure to be in a bustling town again, however, the feel of it was so foreign to me. Being born and raised off the English coastline in a province such as Seaside all my life, the farming community had such differences I may as well have gotten off the steam boat in Katmandu, wherever that is.

Everyone was a bustle to get their crops planted and there was little else talked about. Instead of rows of ships in the harbor there were rows of covered wagons along the road on the outskirts of town. Everyone who are traveling with our party are with their wagons waiting for the signal to strike camp and prepare to hit the trail. We have been delayed due to heavy rains that have caused the roads to be impassable.

The children and I have begun to learn a new language, the language of the pioneer. I do believe I have never used the words strike camp or hit the trail but that is what they call it here in the mid-west of America. They also call our wagons Prairie Boats.

When I asked the men in the mercantile why this was so, they laughed and told me that I would find out soon enough all the while spitting streams of dark juice from their mouths into a copper container on the floor next to them. That I have never seen before. It was enough to make one retch at the sight. I have made it a point to avoid looking in their direction upon my next visit and I thank my good Lord that my husband has not this ugly habit of chewing tobacco.

In the evenings, as we wait for word of our departure, we gather around the central campfire and have worship services. We sing songs of encouragement for our journey through the many dangers of the trail and the wonders of our promised land. It does seem that we have come such a long distance already and we are nowhere near our destination. I am anxious to be on our way so that the unknown of our new life in a covered wagon, as well as our Zion home, will soon be the known and familiar.

Charles has just arrived from the council meeting and informed us that we strike camp at first light and that there will only be a quick prayer instead of a full service tonight then off to sleep to physically prepare ourselves for our first day on the trail. I am sure the excitement will keep us all awake despite the need for rest.

Rachael needed a good night's sleep too, after the events of the past week. She placed the journal back in its box and laid it on her night stand. Turning off the light and snuggling down into her warm bed, she curled her arm around the back of her head and laid there staring at the ceiling. She had pent-up emotions keeping her awake. Fear of the unknown of getting on a plane and flying to a foreign land, like what Elizabeth described, how uncanny the parallel between their lives. Almost as if Elizabeth wrote this journal just to help her with the challenges Rachael had and would face in her life.

Or is it a God thing and he is using Elizabeth's life to show me something for me in my life; showing me Him?

With this thought, she let out a long stream of breath that relaxed her whole body and she dozed off to sleep, letting go of the desire to think about her future. It didn't matter because she had given it to her Father in Heaven.

CHAPTER 17

Rachael hadn't bothered setting an alarm since her bags sat at her door, ready to go. She had been awake at first light since she could remember, and she wasn't meeting Azuno until noon. When she awoke that morning and looked at the clock, however, it read 10:38. She rubbed her eyes and looked again, disbelieving. She had slept in. Jumping out of bed she grabbed her mother's robe along with her shower kit and ran to the bathroom. Fortunately, there were very few students left on campus since many had gone home or elsewhere to celebrate spring break and she had the bathroom to herself.

After a quick shower and brushing of her teeth, she ran back to her room and threw her clothes on from the night before. She didn't have time to do anything with her hair, so she wrapped a scrunchy around her wet curls and called it good as she wrestled her luggage through the door and down the hall to the elevator, then to her car. Before she closed the back hatch, she double checked to see if she had her passport and the traveler's checks she purchased at the bank after her accountant wired her some money.

Everything is as it should be, then why am I so jumpy? I'm so nervous, I feel like I'm forgetting something.... something important. God, are you there? If I need to pay attention to the dread I feel, then please let me know.

Rachael laughed, as she recalled Elizabeth being stressed out and wanting to get on the road. She could relate to Elizabeth's urgency. She just wanted to get there and get back, so she could say she did what God asked of her. She tried to practice obedience. Her independent spirit warred sometimes with authority, but now Rachael could discern a slight shift in her thinking.

Go with Azuno, he is your future.

Alright already I'm going!

When Rachael reached the cafeteria and saw the expression on Azuno's face, she imagined it must mirror her own. Azuno didn't look like he had gotten much sleep the night before. His hair stuck out over his left ear as if he went to bed with it wet and it wouldn't lay flat like the rest. His eyes sunk into his sockets with dark circles under them. He looked nervous as he stood and paced between his chair and the chair he pulled out for her.

He had bought a few breakfast things from what was left in the cafeteria. There, on the table sat a couple of bottles of juice, grapefruit and cran-apple, the least favorite of the students, and doughnuts from yesterday all wrapped up in hopes that they would still be somewhat fresh the next day. Azuno gathered the food up and slipped it into his backpack. He reached his hand out and Rachael placed her small, delicate palm next to his.

"We travel and eat, yes?" Azuno asked and his grip on her hand tightened. Rachael assumed his jitters from his fear of flying were getting to him.

"That's fine. I'm ready if you are." Rachael swung back around and led the way to her car. Azuno followed her and added his bag to hers in the back and closed the hatch. Walking around to the passenger side Azuno's nervousness rose higher in his throat. He counted the times he had been in a car on one hand and never when a woman drove. Reaching for the door handle he noticed his hand shook. He really must get a hold of his nerves.

They had plenty of time to eat their breakfast. The overcast day and a full stomach made Azuno sleepy while riding in the car. The Ancestors had kept him up most of the night arguing about the plans, once they reached Boa Vista.

They did this far into the night until Azuno fell into a fitful sleep just before sun up. When he awoke, he did not remember the final decision. He took comfort in the fact that it must have been decided, and he will only be there in body and not spirit.

The smooth voiced supernatural being had taken over Azuno's body; he could not recognize his own thoughts. They had become one, and Azuno had given in from sheer exhaustion. No man could survive being kept awake for days and be able to resist the strength and intelligence of that dominant voice inside his head. Not even Algebra could side track it last night. The voice reasoned with Azuno and took him around in circles until he just gave in. Everything began to make sense and he no longer cared what would become of them. He just wanted it over.

Azuno crossed his arms in front of him and allowed his head to drop onto his chest in sleep. He did not want to talk to Rachael or look at her. He blocked out memories of her for his own peace of mind. He enjoyed the quiet in the car and the quiet in his head. He wanted peace, now and forever, but he knew it would be short lived.

They arrived at the airport and Azuno pulled Rachael's ticket from his backpack and handed it to her. They had nothing to tag so the woman directed them to the security check where they stood in a line that filled to overflowing the winding, corded off maze.

Azuno had not said anything to Rachael so far and she worried that she had made a big mistake going with him. Where had the smiling friendly Azuno went, the one she had gotten to know back at school? Her heart beat hard against her chest when they were separated at the security desk. Confusing emotions rattled around in her mind.

"Passport please, miss." The security guard at check in asked Rachael. She glanced at Azuno at the other desk and he smiled, reassuring her.

"Why are you visiting Argentina?"

"For spring break, I'm visiting my friend's family there," she replied nodding toward Azuno who had pulled his shoes off and placed them with his bag on the conveyer belt.

"Enjoy your trip," the attendant replied with a smile as he handed her back her plane ticket and passport.

Rachael met Azuno at the end of the conveyer with both bags over his shoulder while she grabbed her shoes out of the grey tub. She slipped them on and caught up to Azuno as he tried to figure out which way to go.

"C gate is this way, Azuno," Rachael said taking hold of his hand this time.

They found their gate and settled into a couple seats near the door where they would board the plane. A sigh escaped Azuno and he dropped his head to his chest.

"So very tired," Azuno explained with a

strange look on his face.

"Flight 1433 to Argentina, now boarding group A, at gate C24. Flight 1433 now boarding at C24," The loud speaker made Rachael jump.

Rachael took a big gulp of air, then another. Azuno reached over and put his arm around her. He pulled her closer and whispered soothing words in his native language, stroking her face as he would a frightened child. It surprised Rachael that he could bring such peace to her troubled thoughts.

When she got up and grabbed her bag to get in line she noticed the change in her, calm and relaxed. She parked that thought in her head to ask him how he did that once they were settled in their seats and in the air, however, when that time came she fell asleep in the window seat next to him.

As the plane descended into Miami they had been in the air for six hours. She had no memory of these hours but Azuno assured her she ate dinner and everything. His concern showed on his face as he pulled her close and stroked her face again for only a few seconds as they waited to change planes. As they walked to the next plane, Rachael's knees buckled. Azuno lifted her pack off her shoulder and wrapped a supportive arm around her waist. She chided herself for being so tired and apologized to him.

"It is good I am here to help. Maybe you need something more to eat or drink."

His eyes searched her face with genuine concern, that made Rachael begin to worry about herself as well.

"I must have jet lag already. Could we sit and rest a minute?" Azuno eased her onto a bench and ran for a bottle of water.

"I'm fine now that I had some water. I feel much better. Please don't worry about me, Azuno. Really, I'll be fine." Rachael assured Azuno. They had only a few minutes before they had to make it across the airport to their next flight connection so Azuno flagged down a cart taxi to carry them and their luggage through the big busy airport.

Back in the plane and settled next to Azuno again, Rachael wanted to talk but her eyelids drooped as the flight attendant went through the emergency procedures. She tried to keep her eyes open, but her lids felt filled with lead. Rachael turned to Azuno and he spoke something soft and comforting as her head bobbed and rested on his shoulder.

Stopping and changing planes took a toll on Rachael. She felt like someone dead walking around in someone else's body. She vaguely recalled getting on the plane in Seattle at 2:30 pm. and now they descended into yet another city. At this point she didn't care if she ever flew again. She just wanted a shower, some coffee, and a nice soft bed.

Azuno had mentioned, as they got off the plane, that they had another lay over for several hours, so she would be able to recover her legs after sitting all night in plane seats. He said there was a lot to see in the village if she was up to venturing from the airport while they waited for their next connection to Buenos Aires later that evening.

"All I want to do is scrub the sweat from my skin and get a coffee. Do you know where I can do that? Then maybe I can think of what I want to do next." Darkness outside made the windows look like mirrors except with a slight tinge of color on the horizon. Azuno directed her to a women's rest room.

"I wait for you here, then to find coffee after," He said as he settled the bags next to the door of the Ladies' room.

He paced back and forth beside the door as the screaming and pounding inside his head began to give him a headache. He no longer understood what was being said, the voices all talked at the same time, talking in different languages he did not understand. He sat against the wall and held his head. His heart skipped around in his chest in fear of their plotting. Azuno thought for a moment that maybe he and Rachael did have some type of illness, maybe even caused by the Ancestors. That realization made his eyes open wide in anticipation of an attack. At that instant he wanted to protect Rachael but when he tried to get to his feet everything went black.

Rachael grabbed some paper towels and shuffled her tired body to the sink. Waiting for warm water with her hand under the faucet she had to accept that it wasn't going to be warm but ice cold. She dampened the paper towels anyway and laid them across her face with a sigh. The cold compress began to revive her. She chided herself for being so weak.

What is wrong with me? I feel like I have lead in my arms and legs. This couldn't be just jet lag, what then?

Sliding the towels away from her tired eyes, she glimpsed a shape coming up behind her in the mirror and turned in time to see a white cotton... something... cover her face. She tried to scream but the cotton filled her mouth. She struggled to pull the hand away that smothered her as bits of the light in the room began to go out and her body went limp as it slid to the floor.

Azuno! Rachael thought she cried out his name, but everything went black.

CHAPTER 18

Sunlight glimmered through maple trees in the back yard of Rachael's house and she could hear squeals of laughter, then her Dad's voice. She peeked around the corner of the house and saw them. She saw her dad pushing her as a little girl in the swing he had made when she was five. And there she was in a bright blue frilly dress pumping her legs pulling the swing higher with her dad pushing her from behind.

"Higher Daddy," the little girl squealed. "Higher."

"Any higher honey and you will land on the moon," her dad laughed.

Rachael reached out and touched something cold and wet which did not register to her mind anything that resembled the dream. She opened her eyes, but she didn't see anything. Frightened now, she reached out with the other hand and felt a cold, hard and wet surface in each direction.

Her mind cleared. What happened? Rachael had difficulty grasping the chain of events that led her here, then a picture of the women's restroom at the airport took shape in her mind. She remembered the person with the black eyes that attacked her in the rest room at the airport. A feeling of panic and dread welled up inside her that made a shiver run down her whole body.

Where am I?

What city did the last plane land in? She had no idea for that strange feeling of just wanting to sleep clouded her memory throughout the flight. Now she had a clear mind, and she wished for the clouds again.

Have I been.... she started breathing in great gulps and the moist, stagnant air gave her no comfort. Reality struck, and her mind began to believe it.

"No, no, no." Rachael screamed with all the air in her lungs. When she gained her breath, she screamed again louder and angrier.

"No. Oh, God no.... God, No. I trusted you and now look at the mess I'm in."

"No. This cannot be happening." Rachael got up on her hands and knees and fumbled around on the straw covered floor to each wall, looking for the opening.

There must be a door, how else could I have gotten in here?

She dug her nails into the rough wood between each board. She could feel a slight variation, but nothing wanted to give in to the pressure from her fingers.

But she felt no difference between each wall. As her eyes adjusted to the darkness she noticed a sliver of light coming from around a door above her. Her prison did not allow her to stand straight but because of that it gave her leverage to push with all her leg strength against the trap door. She pushed until her legs gave out, but it wouldn't budge. With that little bit of light, she could see she was being held in a square cell with walls that were made of rough cut, dark wood of some sort. Then, the walls jerked suddenly and seemed to bob up and down and move as if she floated on water.

"Let me out," she screamed over and over while she pounded her fists against the heavy wood sides. She screamed and pounded until her voice cracked and her hands throbbed with pain from the bruises and scrapes. Standing up as straight as the small space allowed Rachael pressed her eye up to the crack around the trap door to see if she could decipher some clue as to her whereabouts, she could see strange trees and blue sky. Rachael plopped down on the floor of her box and pulled her knees up, rocking herself, sobbing the frustration and fear out of her body.

It hadn't been that long ago that she lived in a perfect world. Not that long ago that she basked in her parents' love, they doted on her. And then, she had begun to feel like there may be some happiness for her with Azuno after her parents' death. But now this?

The thought of never seeing him again, or Aunt Jenny, or the new baby that would bring such joy back to them, overwhelmed her. Her mind began to war with wanting to stay in this world or going to heaven to be with her parents for she believed at that moment it could be very close to what would happen to her. If those were her choices she couldn't choose. She decided to leave it to the Father.

Slowly her sobs lessened, to sighs. Her body sagged with fatigue but with the rocking, she found it difficult to relax. With every up there came a down and side to side. No sound slipped in, no voices, no sound but water whooshing up against the sides of her prison. All accept one faint, rhythmic noise.

She quieted and listened more attentively.

Is that horse's hooves to the left? Then, she heard a whip crack and a groan from an animal she couldn't quite place. Her cell jerked and bumped up then splashed down again. It threw Rachael to the front and then back in her little box which scraped her cheek then elbows as she tried to protect herself from falling. She chose to ride on her hands and knees.

Panic began to cause her to sweat through her pink sweater, and she ripped it over her head putting it under her knees for padding. The air in her tiny world began to close in on her. She wondered if there was enough air coming through the tiny cracks in the roof. She thought about what it would be like to suffocate to death there in that box.

Will this be my coffin? There is not enough air in here.

She lay on her side wrapping her arms around her knees using her sweater for a pillow and relaxed so as not to breathe all the oxygen up too soon. The rhythmic movement, the consistent snap of the whip, and the bumping up then down became the only signal that she continued to live.

What now God? I sure hope you are still in charge here. God, I am so scared. Please God, please help me.

Part of Elizabeth's journal came back to her. The part where they were all locked in the hold of the ship during the storm in the Gulf of Mexico.

I am in a frightening situation, yes, but at least I am only worried about myself and not my children including a brand-new baby. This feels like a storm, but I must trust as Elizabeth and my mother trusted that you are here with me, Father.

"*Yes Rachael, I am here.*"

Peace flooded Rachael like a soft blanket, surpassing all her understanding. She accepted it as a blessed gift. She noticed the difference between her thoughts and His voice. With that peace came rest.

CHAPTER 19

Azuno woke to someone nudging his shoulder. His eyes opened, and he stretched the stiffness out of his back from sleeping on the cold marble floor of the airport hallway next to the Ladies' Room.

"No sleep here," The man that nudged him said in broken English mistaking Azuno for a foreigner.

He stood and looked around, searching for Rachael.

"A woman was with me, an American woman with light hair and blue eyes, did you see her?" He spoke in the Portuguese language of Brazil.

The man in a Security uniform's eyes opened wide when he heard Azuno speak in his native tongue. Then his eyes narrowed as if to assess the situation.

"What are you saying, an American is lost? Why is she traveling with you? Where did you last see her? Why were you sleeping here outside the restroom?"

"She went in and that was the last I saw

of her. We've got to find her, she is in danger," Azuno said as he raced into the ladies restroom with the Security guard following close behind him. He and the guard stood there in disbelief staring down at her backpack on the floor next to the sink. Azuno did not want to believe they had taken her right in front of him. They checked every stall, but they found no sign of her.

Pain flooded Azuno's body which alerted him of something different. The pain came from the emptiness in his soul, his heart, and the dread that he would never see Rachael again. This pain did not come from the Ancestors. He blamed himself for this horrible feeling of loss. Azuno's knees began to shake. He leaned against the wall and slid to the floor holding the last thing Rachael touched, her backpack.

"When did your flight get in?" the guard asked, holding his radio ready to alert the rest of his team of a missing person.

"At sunrise," Azuno answered with a flat, lifeless voice.

He wanted to die if there would be no more Rachael. This thought surprised him, when did he become so intertwined with this woman's life that without her, he would be nothing? He had not realized it because of the control the Ancestors had over his mind. The reality of this dawned like a clear revelation, he couldn't live without her, and that they were meant to be together. The pressure in his chest from the panic and loss overwhelmed him; he buried his face in his hands to cover his pain.

The security guard repeated the information into the radio. A few minutes later, a flurry of activity around him stirred him from his grief. Other uniformed officers took hold of the luggage and escorted him into an office where the one in command offered a seat to Azuno. He fell into the chair, thankful that his weak legs no longer had to hold him up. More questions he could not answer. The airport staff began to unpack their bags on a long table behind Azuno beginning with Rachael's backpack. It didn't matter to Azuno. He knew where she had been taken, but he was powerless to help her now. The Ancestors had left him...... they left him? He listened into his mind. Yes, no voices nor ominous dread came to him. They no longer controlled him. What does that mean for Azuno? He had been so long with them he no longer knew his own mind.

"I know where she has been taken," He said almost to himself in fear that what he suspected about the Ancestors had been just a trick and he would be punished.

Everyone in the room stopped their tasks and turned to him. Over his head the security officer that found him looked at the others.

"What did you say?"

"I know where she has been taken," Azuno repeated louder and leaped to his feet. He could save her; the Ancestors do not know his thoughts now. They could not be one step ahead and punish him.

"We must save her."

The security guard put his hand on Azuno's shoulder and forced him back into his chair.

"Yes, son, we will, but first you have to tell us what happened."

"Hello." Someone knocked on the half-opened door of the office and a face framed in bright red curls came around the corner. Azuno noticed a touch of grey framing the hair that she had swept off her forehead with a clip and slight lines around her mouth and eyes when she smiled.

"The airport manager called and said that I may be of service. He said there was an American woman missing, is that right? Oh, my name is Sally Cooper. I work for the American Embassy," She said as she entered the room and squatted down before Azuno as if she talked to a child.

She laid a hand on Azuno's forearm and left it there, her touch comforted him. The love he felt with that slight touch brought tears to his eyes for the first time in his life, or at least since he buried his mother as a young boy. His father had told him there would be no more tears from that time on. Azuno looked into her soft green eyes and saw such sweetness there.

"We save her, Sally" he said in English wiping his damp eyes.

"I know Azuno, it is time that we do." Sally said with a smile of encouragement that shocked him.

How did she know his name? Was she controlled by the Ancestors too? Fear welled up in his throat, choking him. Sally reached for a glass and the pitcher of water on the desk next to Azuno's chair. She poured a glass and handed it to him.

Azuno gulped it down, hoping the water would ease the pressure in his chest but it didn't. Tiny bits of bitterness that surrounded his heart began to splinter into pieces like broken glass. A vision of her smiling face looking up at him that day in the Math Lab, made the pain worsen. She had just begun to trust him when she had no reason to. All he had taken from her and now this, would he be responsible for taking her life too? His own heart screamed for revenge.

He looked into Sally's eyes again, but only saw light there and not darkness; light like Rachael, light like her Aunt Jenny. He wanted to fall into her arms and sob his fear, his anger, and his loneliness out to her.

"Azuno, I heard as I came to the door that you know where she is. How can we get her back?" Sally asked, leaning against the desk in front of him.

"How you know me?" Fear that the Ancestors would come back into him and cause him pain if he told them what happened almost won out over his fear of never being with Rachael again. He would rather die than be the one that caused her death.

"Oh, we have friends in common my dear," Sally answered his question with a wide smile that reached her sparkling eyes.

"We must go to my village. We must hurry. No time, hurry." Azuno got up and they raced to keep up. The man with the radio began to call for a police escort. Sally said something to the guard that made him put his radio away. As they reached the street, a group of people from Azuno's village that he recognized, stood in a huddle beside the door. Men and women who had disappeared after the mission people came; his people who'd had their souls stolen. Saaju, his friend he traveled with to Boa Vista, separated himself from the crowd and came toward Azuno.

"Azuno, my friend, we want to help. The mission God has sent us to help you get the Blue Eyes back. Come, we take you." Saaju reached out and took hold of the sleeve of his shirt but Azuno pulled back. He knew Saaju worked for his father and he did not want anything to do with him.

Sally intervened for Saaju.

"Wait Azuno, how do you think I know all about what has happened to Rachael? Saaju and the others in Boa who have become friends to the Missionaries in town know things. You know how they know things too, don't you Azuno? I trust them and so should you if you want to get Rachael back. Now let's go. Saaju, we are ready, lead the way," Sally said taking Azuno's hand in hers and led him to a waiting bus that took them to the mountain trails not far from Boa Vista's city limits.

A tiny seed of hope settled into Azuno's heart that maybe they could reach the village in time, even though they must travel through thick jungle and mostly uphill, not to mention that his father's men had a few hours head start. The hope grew when the bus stopped at an airstrip where a helicopter revved up, ready to go. Azuno looked at Sally and she smiled, patting his arm.

Saaju and Sally climbed in first and sat next to a police officer. Azuno took the seat behind them next to another officer. That dreaded old feeling of being in the air came up into Azuno's throat as the engine roared and a cloud of dust flew up as they lifted off the ground. He swallowed his fear, thinking only of Rachael, focusing on the memory of her face smiling up at him the day she nearly knocked him over as she came through the door of the Math Lab. He watched Saaju bow his head and began speaking something. Azuno could hear his strange words in Portuguese.

"Our loving Father in heaven, make our journey swift over this land. Stay the hands of our enemies. Wrap a hedge of protection around the Blue Eyes and keep her safe in your strong tower, in Jesus name, amen."

And Sally repeated that strange word "amen" smiling at Azuno.

"What happened here?" Azuno asked Saaju with harshness that conveyed his confusion and fear.

"Miss Sally and I share the same God and this God is in control. There is a God greater than the Ancestors and He is the Father of Abraham, Isaac, and Jacob; The Father of you too, Azuno, if you should choose his son Jesus."

The sun began to set as the helicopter landed at Saaju's village. Azuno tensed into action as his feet touched the earth, but Saaju held him back.

"No, Azuno, you eat and change for we will need to travel swift and strong." He said looking at Azuno's khaki slacks and converse tennis shoes with severe doubt they would hold up in the jungle.

As they entered the communal hut where everyone gathered for meals and meetings, the women came with platters of food for everyone and Saaju's wife Reema handed Azuno a handful of clothes to wear. Everyone sat down and ate as Saaju filled the newcomers in on what to expect on the trail to reach Rachael and the men that took her.

CHAPTER 20

The bumping and swooshing came to a stop. Rachael had no idea how long she had been locked away or what would happen to her. She had reconciled herself to the idea that death would not be so bad, now that she knew where she would be on the other side. She would be in the arms of her parents, and Elizabeth.

"Okay God, I am trusting you. I'm not exactly sure why, but I guess that's what they call faith, right?" She sighed when she didn't get an answer.

Scraping noises on the other side of her small walled cage alerted her of a change, then the whole box lifted and slammed down. Rachael braced herself against the walls as the box moved forward with a creaking sound, she assumed, the sound came from wheels over rough ground. She hadn't reached her destination like she had thought.

She heard voices only inches from the other side of the wood. Words that seemed familiar to her, but she couldn't understand them. She strained her ears to listen, not even breathing.

As her memory searched for the time where she heard this language, her heart warred with the idea that Azuno spoke this same soft language and her thoughts brought her back to the sofa on the second floor of the cafeteria at school. Azuno had taken her into his arms and cooed soft words in his native tongue.... the native tongue of her captors?

What does this mean?

Rachael couldn't believe that Azuno, who treated her with such sweetness, could have anything to do with this.

"No, I won't believe it. I can't believe it," She said out loud and her voice, which she hadn't used for some time now, cracked, she coughed to clear her throat.

She got back up on her knees and pounded against the wall where she heard the voices.

"Let me out. LET.... ME.... OOOOOUT." She slammed all her weight against the side of the box and it tipped. The voices on the other side of the wall began babbling loud and fast then she heard pounding back, but it sounded like a hammer on nails.

Rachael got onto her feet and threw her weight to one side of the box then to the other side. By this point she didn't care if she turned into a bag of bruises. She wanted more than anything to face her kidnappers and to see for herself what her fate would be. Being taken like this over so many miles, blind to her fate drove her crazy. Crazy and angry enough to split her head open just to be free.

The hammering continued, and the box stopped tipping. Rachael had to give up. She would not gain her freedom any time soon. She slumped down against a wall and resigned herself to her prison for now. She decided that if she rested then maybe she would have the strength to escape once she got out of that blasted box. She leaned her head against the corner and tried to remember some songs she learned in Sunday school.

"Jesus loves me this I know for the bible tells me so......." Rachael sang then realized these soft words made her feel better, just to say Jesus' name. She began to sing stronger.

"Little ones to him belong, they are week, but he is strong.... Yes, Jesus loves me, yes Jesus loves me, yes Jesus love me, the bible tells me so." She sang it again and again until her throat could not sing another note. The creaking and bumping put her in a trance and she whispered "Yes Jesus loves me" to herself repeatedly as if it would be what sustained her.

She hadn't realized they had stopped, she was in such a stupor. Then the trap door opened, and she could see a torch above a bamboo tube that someone poked into the dark box. She heard a breath then smoke filled her cube. She began to choke and cough, she slid down the wall to the floor and blacked out.

CHAPTER 21

Azuno tore through the dark jungle as if his life depended on it, his heart pounding hard against his ribs. Determined to reach Rachael, he began to pull away from the others. It didn't matter. All that mattered was to get to Rachael in time.

Azuno looked back willing the others to keep up. Fear consumed him as if a fire had replaced the blood in his veins. The fear of the Ancestors and their control of the people of his village, especially his own father, warred with the desperate need to get to her. He must take his chances.

Azuno knew he had one advantage over his father; the spirit world of the Ancestors no longer controlled him. How this had happened he had no idea. He knew only that he must push harder and get there faster. He had traveled this path his entire life and had no need of light as his eyes adjusted to the dim glow from a sliver of a moon just above the tree line. Azuno thought of the two separate villages as one since he had spent so much time in both.

The villages practiced independence one from the other in their laws and politics. That gave his father greater influence over his people, he was the law. However, they still depended on each other for trade of goods that skilled individuals made from the resources of their separate areas. That, and for wives. Azuno remembered the women would come looking for husbands, for his village had strong men not damaged by the ways of the foreigners.

Azuno's mind wandered to the politics of his village and the things he hadn't thought peculiar until he had lived among the Americans for the past few months. In America, he saw no man that had more than one wife and that everyone was happy with that arrangement.

Forcing his mind to the present and Rachael, he forged on, looking back on occasion in hopes he hadn't lost the others. Ahead, through the trees, he could see a faint light. He slowed to catch his breath and allow the others to catch up.

Azuno moved silent through the bushes to the break in the trees. He peeked around a tree trunk to see where the light came from. His whole body stiffened as he forced himself to not make a sound for there in the clearing blazed the bonfire from his dream he had back in his small apartment in Bellingham. The clear warning made his hand rub where he wore a welt and his mission now became clear to him.

He watched as the men of his village

chanted and danced around the fire. As he watched, a man made a guttural cry and leaped high in the air over the flames and back to the ground unharmed. Azuno knew the dance, calling the Ancestors to make one brave. The one who leaped the fire disappeared into the Shaman's ceremonial hut beyond the glow of the bonfire. Then another separated himself from the others and leaped and chanted then disappeared into the hut.

A few moments later, as Azuno looked over his shoulder for the others, the chanting stopped. All was silent in the clearing but the crackling of the flames. He turned back in time to see his father come from the hut in full ceremonial costume including the hideous mask handed down to each Shaman for generations; the mask of his people, the Yanomami, the fierce ones.

He tensed as the door of the hut opened and the two men that jumped over the flames came out holding someone between them by the arms. He recognized Rachael even before she struggled, and the blanket fell from her head. He balled both his fists as his resolve cleared his mind. He had decided the only way to free her would be to take her place.

He stepped from the trees as Rachael stood before his father. He took a step as she frantically searched the crowd of men surrounding her. He took another step; it seemed that everyone moved in slow motion. Shazundo reached into his robe and brought out the knife that would take her life.

Rachael screamed and Azuno began running.

"NOOO," he cried out above her voice in English.

Shazundo looked up in surprise as Azuno sped toward him.

Rachael turned and saw Azuno, but she couldn't tell for sure. He looked like the others except he cried out in her language.

The knife arched upward as Azuno raced across the space between them. He stretched out his body and leaped between the knife and Rachael as it came down hard against his chest. Rachael screamed again as Azuno fell at her feet. Blood, his blood splattered across the pink sweater she wore.

Rachael fell at his side as shuffling and running feet gathered all around her. She didn't care what happened to her now. All she cared about was the look on Azuno's face as she cradled him in her arms.

"Rachael, forgive me." Azuno said in a whisper between coughs.

"Shh, don't talk now. I forgive you."

Please God don't let him die for me. He did not need to do this. Please God let him live. He gave his life for me.

Rachael prayed as tears flowed down her face and dripped off her chin onto her hand that held Azuno's.

"I see it, Rachael, love and light," The last words he would say to her on this earth and he chose to talk about the light in her eyes? Rachael held him frantic to keep him alive.

"Someone, please help me," she cried out as she tried to stop the bleeding. Then his body slumped in her arms and she crumpled over him crying great sobs of all that would never be.

Rachael didn't know how long she had been there next to Azuno's motionless body, but a woman spoke English to her and helped her up. Then there were men all around her, some in uniform and others dressed as the tribe's people, the woman dragged her away from Azuno, the fire, and all that she had been through the past two days.

"No, I want to stay with Azuno." She sobbed and gasped for breath. "Please. Let me go back to him. He needs me." Rachael tried to pull away from the grasping arms that dragged her from Azuno. She turned her head and looked for him lying in the circle of light thrown off by the fire, but she couldn't see him, too many people blocked her view.

"Honey, he's gone. We must get you to safety before the Shaman brings back the others. We must hide you and get you out of the country, back where you belong." Sally said in her take charge voice that everyone seemed to submit to.

As the terror she woke to after the smoke induced sleep forced on her in the box slipped back into her mind she submitted to being taken to safety. Her body shook from the trauma of being tied to a post in a hut like those in her dream when she watched her parents being stabbed to death in their sleep. Her terror heightened when a cloth flap flew open and this petrifying monster with giant horns and fangs and grass hair down to his knees covering a robe of leopard fur came into the room. She knew she would die soon.

As the scenes of the last moments she had with Azuno flew back into her mind, she looked down at her hands. Even in the dim light of the moon she could still see the blood on them, his blood. Her stomach flopped upside down in her body as she reeled on her feet and passed out. "He's gone; he's gone" echoed in her mind as everything went black.

CHAPTER 22

As Rachael drove back to school, what should have been her sophomore year, she scrolled through the well-worn memories of Azuno she used to calm her sadness. Something she had begun to enjoy, the memories of Azuno, all she had left of him. The memories of her parents, all she had left of them, so she combed over these fond memories every chance she had. The long drive from Spokane to Bellingham she chose as her special time with the loved ones she had lost.

It had been yet another painful chapter in her life once she arrived back in the states. The American Embassy in Boa Vista had called Uncle Ben and Aunt Jenny the moment they went searching for her. While Sally and Azuno raced toward the village where she had been taken, Uncle Ben had made arrangements for Aunt Jenny to fly in to meet him in Seattle and to wait for Rachael to come home.

When Rachael got off the plane she had fallen into Aunt Jenny's arms, again with a broken heart. When Azuno died in her arms, her heart broke because she loved him. Loved him more than she had ever loved another, different from her parents. This love she had waited for, the love that would allow her to give up her independence, now gone as swiftly as the knife that sliced through his chest.

The memory of Azuno's sacrifice carried her through the grief. Going back to the campus where they fell in love she hoped would revive the sweeter memories; memories of their first touch, where he smiled and laughed.

Why send him to me then take him away? What will be my future now without him? There is so much I still don't understand.

A thought flew through her mind then disappeared. She barely grasped it as it took flight. She had seen herself as a missionary with native children all around her laughing.

A missionary like my parents, hmmm? Rachael shrugged her shoulders and stored that information in the back of her mind for future reference as she drove down I-90 west.

She had spent hours, while recovering from her trip to South America, reading Elizabeth's journey through the US to finally arrive at her Zion. She described the vast grass lands that reach from one horizon to the other. Grass as high as the bed of the wagon and she finally figured out why they called the wagons Prairie Boats. As Elizabeth looked back at the others traveling along the grasslands, the wagons seem to float along on the top of the grass like on the sea. And when the wind blew, the tall green grass flowed with it like waves upon an ocean.

Her family was strong and healthy throughout the journey; even baby Eliza Golconda, the blessed baby that survived everything by the grace of God. Elizabeth had found her Zion. Paradise. Holy Land. Is there such a thing on this earth anymore? And just as it ended for Adam and Eve, could it last?

The summer months she spent with Aunt Jenny, Sam and Shelly, and the new adorable little cherub Nathan Michael, named after Rachael's Dad, with his chubby cheeks and sweet blue eyes, made it easier for her to forget the past.

A flash of light. Mumbled voices scraped at the edges of consciousness. Beeping of equipment nagged away at the storms raging inside. As if from the bottom of a dark lake all things began to come into focus as the surface neared.

With a heart beating through the pain in his chest, he began to pant.

"Rachael!"